TWINTUITION
DOUBLE CROSS

TIA AND TAMERA MOWRY

TWiNTUiTiON
DOUBLE CROSS

HARPER
An Imprint of HarperCollinsPublishers

Library of Congress Control Number: 2017949430
ISBN 978-0-06-237296-3

Typography by Carla Weise
22 23 24 25 26 PC/BRR 10 9 8 7 6 5 4 3 2 1
❖
First paperback edition, 2022

*I dedicate this book to my incredible children,
Cree and Cairo, and my lovely and
supportive husband, Cory.*
—Tia

*To my entire family—my mother, Darlene; father,
Timothy; my brothers, Tahj and Tavior; sister, Tia;
husband, Adam; son, Aden; and daughter, Ariah.*
—Tamera

1
CAITLYN

"MAYBE WE SHOULD text Grandmother Lockwood again," I said. "She might text us back if we tell her what I saw in my last vision."

My twin sister, Cassie, shot a cautious look toward the kitchen. Our mother was in there puttering around with something on the stove, humming under her breath. "We can talk about it later," Cass murmured, miming a lip-zip.

I sighed and leaned back on the sofa. It was Monday afternoon. Cass and I had come home from school about half an hour earlier, and Mom was supposed to leave for work right after dinner. It made sense to wait.

Cassie shot another look toward Mom, who was paying no attention to us. Then she mimed unzipping her lips.

"Anyway, we shouldn't be in such a hurry for Granny L to come back," she said quietly, grabbing the remote and turning up the volume on the goofy celebrity gossip show she was watching. "She might convince Mom not to let us go on the class trip."

I picked at my cuticles, thinking about that. The sixth-grade class trip to San Antonio was just three days away. It would be the first time Cassie and I had been back to our old hometown since Mom had landed a job on the police force in tiny Aura, Texas.

But a lot had happened in that couple of months. For one thing, Cassie and I had actually become friends again. Everyone said we looked exactly alike, from our big brown eyes to our skinny legs. But the thing was, we were very different in all kinds of other ways. That had made us drift apart for a while.

Then, shortly after the move, we'd discovered something weird. As in, *really* weird. We were both having crazy visions!

It happened when we touched someone. Oh, not every time—thank goodness for that! But we never knew when it might happen. All we had to do was brush up against someone, and we might suddenly find ourselves right smack in the middle of a vision about that person.

A vision of the future.

I know that sounds totally wackadoodle. But it was true! Grandmother Lockwood had confirmed it. She was our dad's mom, and we hadn't known she existed until she sent us a package with some family heirlooms in it for our twelfth birthday—and then showed up on our doorstep herself! She'd explained that Cass and I had inherited something called the Sight. It ran in the Lockwood family—our dad had had it, too.

Speaking of our dad, Mom had always told us he'd died when we were too young to remember. We'd had no reason to doubt that story until recently. Then I'd had another vision. It had showed our grandmother standing on a hilly street, embracing a man who looked an awful lot like the one and only picture we'd ever seen of our dad.

Needless to say, I really, really wanted to talk to Grandmother Lockwood about that vision. But she'd left town without telling us where she was going or when she'd be back. The only thing she had told us was not to go on the class trip. She didn't say why—just that it could be dangerous. Scary, right?

Not that I was thinking much about the trip right then. I stared at the TV, where some boy band was dancing around.

"I just wish . . . ," I began.

The shrill ring of the house phone interrupted me. Yes, Mom is still old-fashioned enough to have a landline. I leaned over and grabbed the cordless handset from the coffee table.

"Hello, Waters residence, Caitlyn speaking," I said.

"Cait?" The voice on the other end of the line sounded muffled but familiar. "Is your mother there?"

"Aunt Cheryl?" For a second I wasn't sure it was Mom's sister. She sounded weird—sort of tense. "Hi, funny you should call right now," I said. "Cass and I were just talking about San Antonio—you know, our class trip is—"

"Cait, I really need to talk to Deidre," Aunt Cheryl cut me off. "Is she there?"

"Um, sure, hang on." I raised my eyebrows at Cassie as I lowered the phone. "Hey Mom, Aunt Cheryl's on the phone!"

"Thanks." Mom bustled out of the kitchen and took the phone. "Cheryl? I don't have much time to talk, I have to . . ."

Her voice trailed off as she listened to whatever her sister was saying. Then she abruptly turned away and hurried toward her bedroom. A second later we heard the door click shut.

"That was weird." I stared toward the hallway leading to the bedrooms. "Aunt Cheryl sounded kind of—"

"Quiet!" Cassie ordered, suddenly leaning forward. She cranked up the volume on the TV another few notches.

I glanced at the picture. A reporter was talking, looking excited. Behind her was a headshot of a pretty young Asian woman with blue streaks in her hair.

"Is that Sakiko Star?" I asked.

Cassie shushed me again. I took that as a yes. Sakiko was Cassie's favorite singer these days. I liked her music just fine, but I wasn't that interested in celebrity gossip.

The story was about some escalating feud between Sakiko and her eccentric billionaire neighbor. The reporter looked super excited as she talked about how the guy was dumping his trash in the Dumpster that Sakiko had rented for a home renovation project.

". . . and while Mr. Jeffers denies everything," the reporter went on breathlessly, "the definite clues are parrot poop and a lot of empty sardine cans."

"Sardine cans?" I echoed with a laugh. "Really, that's a clue?"

"Uh-huh." Cassie's eyes were locked on the TV screen. "Apparently the neighbor guy always smells like fish."

I snorted. Then I blinked as a picture of two neighboring mansions popped up on the screen. One of them looked a bit shabby—a few windows were boarded up, and the yard and shrubs were all overgrown.

But I was focused on the other house. "Wait, why does that place look familiar?" I said slowly, trying to figure it out.

Cassie shrugged. "Duh. That's Sakiko's place. You've probably seen it on TV."

"Oh." The picture cut away to a video of Sakiko singing onstage. I still had a nagging little feeling that the house was familiar somehow. But I figured my sister was probably right—she was always watching stuff about Sakiko online and on TV. I'd probably seen the star's house a dozen times without really taking it in, and now it was lodged in my brain along with a zillion other useless bits of trivia.

Losing interest, I headed toward the bathroom. It was down the narrow hall that led off the living room to the rest of the house. Mom's bedroom came first, and as I passed, I could hear her on the phone even through the closed door. She sounded kind of upset.

That was even weirder than Aunt Cheryl's behavior on the phone. Deidre Waters wasn't the type of person who got upset by much. Otherwise, she wouldn't have survived her many years in the military, let alone the police academy. Sure, she yelled at Cassie and me sometimes, especially when Cass missed curfew or I forgot to put my dirty clothes in the hamper. But getting angry or annoyed or exasperated wasn't the same as getting *upset*.

I paused by the door, torn between guilt and curiosity. Aunt Cheryl called all the time—she and Mom were close. But today had seemed different. It was obvious she hadn't just called to chat and catch up, or she would have talked to me for a while before asking for Mom. And Mom wouldn't have locked herself in her room to talk to her.

So what was going on?

I couldn't resist leaning a little closer. The doors in our house were thin, but Mom's voice was pretty muffled. Still, I could hear a few words here and there—something about a key chain, and then "It can't be" and "He's dead, Cheryl. I made my peace with that years ago."

I gulped, flashing back again to that vision. What if it was true? What if my dad really was still alive? But how could Aunt Cheryl possibly know that, if Mom and Grandmother Lockwood had no idea?

Suddenly I realized that Mom's voice had stopped. I jumped away from the bedroom door and reached for the bathroom knob. A split second later, Mom burst out of her room.

She spotted me standing there. I guessed maybe I looked guilty, because her eyes narrowed.

"Um, hi," I said as cheerfully as I could manage. "How's Aunt Cheryl?"

"Fine." Mom's voice was almost a growl. She strode past me into the bathroom. The door slammed shut behind her, and the lock clicked.

2

CASSIE

"SHOULD I GET these shoes?" Lavender Adams tod-dled out from behind a rack of dresses with her feet shoved into a pair of serious stilettos. My friends and I were browsing in one of Aura's nicest bou-tiques. Okay, there are only, like, three decent shops in the entire tiny town. But this was definitely one of them.

I shook my head. "For the trip? Not unless you want to bring home a busted ankle as a souvenir."

Megan March snorted with laughter. "Good one, Cass!"

Lav looked less amused. "Actually, I was thinking ahead to the winter dance," she said with a sniff. "I already have plenty of nice clothes for the trip."

Lav hates being laughed at. But whatever. I was too focused on my own shopping to worry about her ego. I had plenty of clothes, too. But I wanted to make sure I wore something special this time.

My cheeks went hot as I thought about the reason why. Namely, Brayden Diaz. He was the cutest guy in the sixth grade, and also the star of the middle school football team. Well, normally he was, anyway. He'd broken his leg in a game that fall and was still on crutches.

I still felt a little guilty about that broken leg. Because I'd seen it happen in a vision—only I hadn't realized that until it was too late to stop it from happening in real life. Actually, back then Caitlyn and I hadn't been sure we *could* stop the stuff we saw. We hadn't known why our brains shorted out now and then, showing us weird little scenes that didn't make much sense.

But now we knew more about the visions. We knew they showed the future, and that they ran in our family. We'd also figured out that we could sometimes change the things we saw. Too bad it was way too late for Brayden's leg by then . . .

"Hey Cass, what about this?" Megan held up a cute pair of purple leggings. "You look amazing in this color."

"Thanks." I took the leggings and held them up against myself, then glanced toward the full-length mirror by the dressing room. As usual, Megan had great taste. That was one of the reasons we'd become such good friends.

The salesgirl had been playing with her phone behind the counter, but now she looked up. "Fabulous!" she declared. "They're very you, Cassie."

That's the thing about living in an itty-bitty town like Aura. Everyone knows everyone else. I still wasn't sure if I liked that or not.

"Thanks," I called to the salesgirl, who had already gone back to staring at her phone. Then I examined myself in the mirror. "It could work. Maybe with my gray striped tunic and a pair of flats."

"Yeah. That sounds comfy for walking around all day." That was Abby, one of the minions.

Caitlyn thinks it's rude for me to call them that, but it's just the truth. See, there's Megan, the most popular girl in school. She's blond and perfect, and her family pretty much rules Aura. Then there's Lav, her second in command since kindergarten. And me—their new BFF. Finally, there are Abby and Emily and a few others who hang around us, aka: minions.

"We're going to be walking around a lot?" Emily looked up from flipping through a pile of colorful T-shirts.

"Duh." Lavender rolled her eyes. "Didn't you pay attention to the announcements this morning? They said to wear comfortable shoes." She kicked off the stilettos and put them back on the shelf.

"Have you been to the Alamo before, Cassie?" Megan asked me.

I nodded. "Sure, a few times," I said. "It's pretty cool."

"Some old building?" Lav wrinkled her nose. "If you say so. Personally I'm psyched about the free time afterward."

"Yeah, they said we're allowed to wander around

River Walk and do whatever we want." I'd been to San Antonio's popular pedestrian walkway plenty of times, too. But I was looking forward to showing my new friends around my old stomping grounds.

"River Walk sounds sort of romantic." Lav smirked at me. "Maybe you and Brayden can spend some quality time together. I mean, that's the point of y'all being partners, right?"

Her hazel eyes were a little sharp. She'd had a crush on Brayden before getting together with his friend Biff recently.

"Or maybe not," I said. "My sister is our partner too, remember?"

I frowned at the thought. Everyone was supposed to sign up for the trip with a buddy, and Brayden had asked me to be his. Super sweet, right?

Only Caitlyn had spaced out and forgotten to find a buddy. Her two nerdy friends, Liam and Bianca, were signed up together, and most other people also had partners. So, the teachers had decided to stick her with me and Brayden! Lame, right?

"It kind of makes sense." Megan was peering down into a case with sunglasses and stuff in it.

"I mean, he's on crutches. Like Principal Zale said, it will be good to have two of you helping him get around."

"Whatever," I muttered. Leave it to Megan to look on the bright side. She was almost as bad as my sister that way.

As for me, I wasn't feeling particularly chipper about the whole deal. Okay, so maybe Caitlyn and I were getting along better than we had in years. That didn't mean I wanted her third-wheeling it around San Antonio with me and Brayden.

But I was trying not to let it bug me. It wasn't as if Caitlyn had done it on purpose. She was no more thrilled about it than I was.

Besides, there was Granny Lockwood's warning about the class trip being dangerous. So maybe it was better if Cait and I stuck together, just in case . . .

"What about this?" Lavender's excited yelp interrupted my thoughts.

She'd just slipped on a baby blue bomber jacket. It actually looked pretty good with her brown hair and rosy cheeks.

"Hang on—the collar's messed up." I hurried over to fix it for her.

As my hand brushed Lav's neck, I stiffened. The Lav right in front of me had suddenly gone pale and distant, like a faded old photograph. In her place was another Lav. She was indoors—that was about all I could tell, since the background was fuzzy and dim. But Lav herself was plenty vivid. She was screaming as someone—I couldn't see who—yanked her cell phone out of her hand, smashed it under a booted foot, and then shoved her through a darkened doorway . . .

"Cassandra!" a sharp voice barked out.

I gasped as Lavender turned to see who had called my name, breaking the connection. Whoa! The vision had taken me by surprise. Luckily none of my friends seemed to have noticed anything unusual. That was just one of the not-so-hot things about the visions. We went all spacey when they were happening, which tended to bring on a lot of awkward questions.

Then I blinked, wondering if I was still lost in

some alternative world. Because my grandmother was suddenly striding toward me, dressed in one of her usual rich-old-lady skirt suits, with her silver hair piled tidily atop her head. Caitlyn was trailing along behind her, looking worried.

"G-grandmother Lockwood?" I stammered, trying to catch up to what was happening.

Megan's eyes widened. "This is your grandma?" She looked from Granny L to me and back again. I couldn't blame her for being confused—I'd never told my friends that my dad was white. What can I say? It hadn't ever come up.

Grandmother Lockwood barely spared a glance for my friends. "Come with me—now," she ordered in her crisp British accent, crooking one long, bony finger at me.

"What? Why?" I clutched the purple leggings. "I'm kind of in the middle of something right now."

"Whatever it is, it can wait." She sounded grim. But then again, she usually sounds like that. Still, there was something different about her attitude this time. My heart skipped a beat as I thought about that vision of Cait's—the one where she thought she'd seen our dad . . .

"It's okay, Cass." Megan grabbed the leggings out of my hand. "I'll put these on my card, and you can pay me back."

"Th-thanks." I barely had time to smile at Megan before Caitlyn was yanking me toward the shop door. Lav and the minions looked confused.

"Uh, bye?" Lav's voice floated after me.

Moments later we were in the hired limo that Granny L always rode around in when she was in Aura. The driver greeted me cheerfully, then started the engine.

"When did you get back?" I asked my grandmother, sinking into the plush leather seat beside Cait. "What's going on?"

"She just flew in today—she picked me up at my student council meeting on her way from the airport." Caitlyn's hand strayed up to touch the key-shaped pendant hanging on a thin chain around her neck.

That necklace was one of the gifts Grandmother

Lockwood had given us. It was an old family heirloom, but it was more than that. It was a talisman—it made our visions stronger when we were wearing it. Sometimes that was a good thing, and sometimes not so much. Caitlyn and I had pretty much settled into a pattern of trading off once a day or so, and today it was her turn to wear it. That was probably why I hadn't been able to see much of the background in my vision about Lav just now.

I frowned, flashing back to the vision. Caitlyn and I had figured out that her visions only predicted good stuff, while I only saw bad stuff. So, what kind of bad stuff had I just seen happening to Lavender?

Before I could figure it out, Grandmother Lockwood leaned over and slid the glass window shut, separating us from the driver. "I've just had some news," she said. "There seems to be some new evidence that your father"—she took a deep breath and closed her eyes for a second—"that your father might still be alive."

3
CAITLYN

"WHOA!" MOM LOOKED startled when Cassie, Grandmother Lockwood, and I burst into the house a few
minutes later. "Where's the fire?" Then she paused,
frowning. "Oh. Verity. You're back."

I winced. Mom and Grandmother Lockwood
aren't exactly the best of buddies. Maybe it's because
Mom kept the whole Lockwood side of the family a
secret from Cass and me all these years—especially
the part about the Sight. Or maybe it's like in the
movies, where mothers- and daughters-in-law just

don't ever seem to get along. Either way, things could be a little tense whenever the two of them were in the same room. Or even the same zip code.

"She just got back from England," I explained.

"Yeah. And she's got huge news!" Cassie added.

"*Good* news." I shot a look toward Grandmother Lockwood. She looked upset, which seemed a little strange. I mean, her son might be alive instead of dead! So why wasn't she doing a happy dance?

Okay, maybe she wasn't the happy dance type. But she could at least look a little more cheerful about what she'd just told us, right?

"There's much to discuss," Grandmother Lockwood said, still grim. "My people back in the UK have recently discovered some interesting information . . ."

"Our dad might be alive!" I blurted out. I couldn't help it. Even after fretting over my vision for the past few days, I still could hardly believe it might be true. Talk about amazing!

Mom's eyes widened slightly. Then her frown deepened. "What are you talking about?" Her voice was a little rough around the edges. "John died years ago. You know that." She glared at Grandmother Lockwood. "What tall tales are you feeding these girls now?"

The older woman sighed. "I don't know what's going on myself yet, Deidre," she said. "But our investigators seem to think that John's death might have been"—she paused and cleared her throat—"faked."

Cassie nodded. "Plus Cait saw him in a vision a few days ago." She poked me in the side. "Tell them."

"It happened when I touched Cassie's hand the other day," I explained. "I saw her standing in a street—I'm not sure where. It didn't look familiar or anything. I mean, I don't think it was here in Aura, or in San Antonio either, since the sidewalks looked different and—"

"Get on with it, Cait!" Cassie interrupted.

"Oh. Right." I do that when I'm freaked out sometimes—talk and talk without really saying anything. I just can't stop myself.

But now I took a deep breath, trying to recall the details of the vision. Suddenly Cass poked me again.

"Oh!" I blurted out. "Um, right. So, Cassie was watching while Grandmother Lockwood hugged someone." I shot Mom a look, wondering how she was taking this. "A man. Um, he looked like that picture Cassie and I saw once—the one of you and our dad at your wedding?"

Mom blanched. "I see," she said after a moment. "Girls, I realize this whole Sight thing must be very unnerving for you." As she spoke, her voice changed from Confused Mom to Officer Waters—efficient and emotionless. "But you shouldn't jump to conclusions. That photo is old, and you saw it a long time ago. And a lot of people look similar."

"Yeah, but that's not the only time we've seen the same guy," Cassie put in, sounding kind of aggressive. "He's been in a couple of other visions lately. Why would we be having these random visions about some guy who just sort of looks like our dad?"

Random was right. Normally Cass and I only saw visions that involved the person we were touching. That applied to a couple of the visions about maybe-our-dad. The one I'd just described had come on when I'd touched Cassie's hand, and she'd been in the vision, too. Another one had happened when I'd put my arm around Mom. That one had showed Mom with the guy at Christmastime.

But there had been a third vision about him. And that time, no one Cassie and I knew had been in the vision at all. Just maybe-Dad and another man we'd never seen before talking in an unfamiliar bedroom. Maybe-Dad had handed the other guy something we couldn't really see, and then the other guy had left. Weird, right?

Anyway, Grandmother Lockwood seemed to think we'd had that vision because Cassie and I were touching some other family talismans—objects that had been in the Lockwood family for generations. Supposedly they had absorbed the energy from every vision a person had while touching them. Or something like that. I still didn't understand how it all worked, but I wasn't too worried about it right then.

"Let's not get off track, ladies," Grandmother Lockwood said. "As I mentioned, my investigators have uncovered some new information."

"Investigators?" Mom echoed with dismay. "Why would you suddenly start poking into John's death after all these years?"

Grandmother Lockwood walked over and set her purse on the table. Then she sat down, carefully smoothing her skirt over her knees.

"It wasn't sudden," she said. "We've been looking into the situation since it occurred. You must admit, Deidre, John's disappearance was a bit . . . odd, hmm?" She stared at Mom, as if daring her to say otherwise.

Mom looked surprised. "Wait. Are you telling me you've been looking into it all this time?"

"So how did he die?" I asked, realizing they still hadn't told us. "Or, you know, fake-die, or whatever."

"Let's not get into that right now." Mom sounded firm.

Cassie rolled her eyes. "Okay, then what did the investigators find?" She glanced at Grandmother Lockwood. "You said you'd tell us when we got here."

"So I did." Grandmother Lockwood nodded. "The investigators have recently been following some online chatter they thought might be related to John, which raised the idea of a faked death. In the meantime, they also found some old, partially destroyed letters between John and someone else, who signed only with the initials QJ."

"QJ?" I said. "Who's that?"

"I have no idea." Grandmother Lockwood sounded annoyed. I got the feeling she wasn't used to not knowing stuff. "But things are happening, and between that and your recent visions, well, it seems the case may be coming to a head. Which is why I hurried back—I wanted to make sure you two aren't still thinking of going to San Antonio this week."

"What?" Mom said. "The class trip? Why wouldn't they go?"

"It could be dangerous," Grandmother Lock-wood said. "The city was mentioned in some of the online chatter—we're not sure why."

"What kind of chatter?" Cassie demanded. "And why would they talk about San Antonio? Our father never lived there." She glanced at Mom. "Did he?"

"No, he didn't." Mom was frowning again. "In any case, I don't think any of this so-called information sounds like reason enough for the girls to miss their class trip."

"But, Deidre . . . ," Grandmother Lockwood began.

Mom shook her head. "But nothing," she cut her off. "I won't let this Lockwood craziness completely control our family. The girls deserve to have fun with their friends." She shrugged. "And just to make sure everything is kosher, I've decided to tag along to San Antonio myself."

"What?" Cassie, Grandmother Lockwood, and I all blurted out at the same time.

"I've volunteered to be a chaperone for the trip." Mom shrugged again. "I was going to tell you two this afternoon."

Cassie and I traded a glance. She looked surprised, just like me, and also kind of dismayed. When we were little, we used to pretend we could read each other's minds—we called it twintuition.

But I didn't need anything extra-sensory to guess what my sister was thinking right then. She was picturing Officer Mom shutting down any and all fun—especially the kind that might involve a certain cute football player . . .

But then Cass shrugged. "Okay," she said. "So we can go? It's final?"

Grandmother Lockwood opened her mouth, but Mom didn't let her get a single word out. "Yes," she said firmly. "It's final."

I YAWNED AS Mom pulled her car into the school parking lot on Thursday morning. The sun was barely peeping into view on the horizon, and my eyes were having trouble staying open.

"I can't believe we had to wake up even earlier than usual," I mumbled.

Cassie rolled her eyes. She's a morning person—just one more thing we don't have in common.

"Get over it," she told me. "You can sleep in tomorrow, okay?"

I perked up a little, realizing she was right.

Tomorrow was an in-service day, which meant the teachers had to show up at school but the students had the day off.

"Yeah, three-day weekend," I said. "Actually four-day weekend, sort of, if you count today, right?"

Cassie wasn't paying attention. She was peering out the window as Mom pulled into a free space. "There's Megan," she said. "I'm going to go say hi."

She was out of the car almost before Mom cut the engine. I glanced out the window and saw a bunch of kids milling around near a pair of yellow school buses.

My friends were among them. The two of them wandered over when they saw me climb out of the car. Liam O'Day was one of the first people I'd met in Aura, and I'd liked him right from the start. He was smart and friendly and a little nerdy. A lot nerdy, according to my sister. But I liked that about him. It meant he was curious and smart and enthusiastic, and lots of other good stuff.

His friend, Bianca Ramos, was quickly becoming a good friend of mine, too. She was a lot quieter than Liam, walking around school with her nose in a book half the time. But she was a talented musician and really interesting once you got to know her.

"Hi, Caitlyn," Liam greeted me cheerfully. "Good morning, Mrs. Waters. Did you come to see us off?"

"Not exactly," Mom replied.

"She's one of our chaperones," I told my friends.

"Oh!" Bianca looked surprised. "You didn't tell us, Caitlyn."

She was right, I hadn't. For some reason, I'd spent the last day and a half thinking that maybe Mom wouldn't actually go—that it was all an excuse to get Grandmother Lockwood off our case. But here she was, wearing her most comfortable shoes, so I guessed that meant it was for real.

Mom shot me a look. "It was a last-minute decision," she told my friends. Then she glanced at her watch. "Excuse me. I'd better go check in."

She hurried off toward the little cluster of adults near one of the buses. "We signed up to be on the same bus as you and Cassie," Liam told me.

"Cool." I was still kind of annoyed to be stuck

with my sister and her crush as my trip buddies. Probably not as annoyed as Cassie, but still.

We headed over to our bus. Ms. Church, the math teacher, was there checking off names on a clipboard. Mom seemed to be assigned to the other bus—she was over with Principal Zale and a couple of other teachers.

"Liam, Bianca, go ahead." Ms. Church waved my friends aboard. I started to follow them, but only got one step up before the teacher stopped me with a hand on my arm. "Hold on, Miss Waters, where's your partner?" She checked the list more carefully. "Er, partners?"

"I think they're coming now." I shaded my eyes against the rising sun. Cassie and her cluster of friends were moving toward us. It was easy to spot Brayden among them. For one thing, he was pretty tall. Besides that, he was the only one on crutches.

When they reached the bus, Cassie pushed past the others to Brayden's side. "This is our bus, right?" she asked Ms. Church. "Come on, Brayden."

"Careful, Mr. Diaz." Ms. Church held out a hand

to stop Cassie. "Go ahead—Caitlyn can help you up the steps."

I gulped, shooting an apologetic glance toward my sister. But what could I do? Brayden was already handing the teacher his crutches. Then he reached for my hand.

As soon as I grasped his hand in mine, the vision took over. All I could hear was the usual buzzing sound in my head. The real Brayden faded away, replaced by a brighter version of him. In the vision, this Brayden was lying flat, splayed out on a brick walkway, looking breathless and disheveled, with his crutches lying askew, just out of reach.

"Hey!" Brayden pulled his hand away, then steadied himself on the bus railing. He laughed. "Yo, Caitlyn, are you trying to let me fall down the steps so you can have Cassie all to yourself as your trip buddy?"

I forced a laugh, doing my best to banish the weird spacey feeling that always hung around after a vision. "Sorry," I said. "I guess I just lost my balance. I'm not a morning person."

Brayden grinned. "Let's try again . . ."

This time we both managed to get up the steps. Brayden collapsed into an empty seat near Liam and Bianca. I slid into the seat across from him, figuring Cassie would want to sit with Brayden.

Meanwhile Ms. Church had climbed aboard, still holding Brayden's crutches. "Here you go, Mr. Diaz," she said. "Why don't you lean them against the window? The twins can sit across from you here." The teacher waved a hand toward me.

Cassie came up behind the teacher just in time to hear her words. She scowled at me, obviously blaming me for the whole deal. But Brayden had already scooted out to the aisle side of his seat, wedging the crutches in between him and the window. So, Cassie had no choice but to flop down next to me.

"Sorry," I whispered. But if she heard me, she didn't let on. Instead she waved to the rest of her friends, who were climbing aboard.

"Woo-hoo!" shouted a tall kid named Biff, pumping his fist. "Let's get this show on the road!"

His friends Brent and Buzz cheered. The three

of them, along with Brayden, were known around school as the B Boys. They were all on the football team together.

Biff and Buzz ended up right behind me and Cassie, while Megan and Lavender sat down across from them. I noticed that Brent was sitting with a kid from my homeroom named Gabe Campbell.

"Whoa," I whispered to Cassie. "Are Brent and Gabe trip buddies? How'd that happen?"

This time she actually responded. "Ugh, Brent lost a bet," she whispered back. "I guess it happened during that whole Truth or Dare craze last week."

I shuddered, feeling a little sorry for Brent. Gabe's uncle was the whole reason my family had ended up in Aura. He'd been on the police force, but then someone had caught him embezzling money. When he got kicked out, that had opened up a job for someone else—namely, our mom.

Cassie and I hadn't known about all that at first. Actually, Mom hadn't really known that much about it, either. But Gabe had, and he'd had it out for Cass and me since we'd arrived in town.

Still, maybe Gabe had done Cassie a favor this time. If he hadn't insisted on being partners with Brent, then Brent probably would have signed up with Brayden. Then I thought of something even worse. If nobody else had been partners with Gabe, I might have been stuck with him myself! I like to see the good in everybody, but even I couldn't find much to like about Greasy Gabe, as Cassie liked to call him.

Luckily, Gabe and Brent were two seats away, so I didn't worry about him for long. I stood up to talk to Liam and Bianca, who were in front of me.

"This is going to be fun, right?" I said.

"Definitely!" Liam sounded excited. "Did you know that the Alamo was once owned by some guy who used it as part of his wholesale grocery business? That was only forty years after the famous Battle of the Alamo . . ."

There was more, but I was only half listening. Lavender was standing, too, leaning forward to talk to Cassie.

"So I looked it up," Lavender said. "That Viral

Vinyl place is only, like, six blocks from where they're dropping us off for free time. Megan and Biff and I are going to sneak away and check it out. Want to come?"

"Sure, I'm in," Cassie replied.

When Lavender sat down to talk to Megan, I sat down, too. "Are you really going to sneak off?" I asked my sister quietly.

She shrugged. "Want to come? I mean, technically we're kind of stuck together, right?" She sounded less than thrilled. "But anyway, Lav's plan will make it easier to meet up with Steve."

"Steve? You mean our cousin Steve?" Steve was Aunt Cheryl's only kid. He was a year older than Cassie and me. When we'd all lived in the same neighborhood in San Antonio, we'd hung out with him all the time.

"Of course I mean Cousin Steve," Cassie said. "I texted him to come straight home from school today so we can meet up with him."

"Why?" I said. "I mean, I'm always happy to see Steve. But we're not really supposed to leave the group."

Cassie glanced around to make sure nobody was listening to us. "I want to find out more about that vision you had—the one about Mom and Aunt Cheryl and the shiny little thingamabob. Remember?"

A few days ago, I'd touched Mom and had one of my strongest visions yet. It had showed Mom and Aunt Cheryl standing in the front hallway of Aunt Cheryl's house. They'd been looking at something in Mom's hand, though I hadn't been able to see what it was—just that it was small and shiny. Aunt Cheryl had her arm around Mom, who was shaking and crying. Which was so not like Mom at all . . .

"Okay," I said slowly. "But that vision hasn't happened yet, right? I mean, Mom hasn't been back to San Antonio since you had it."

"Not that we know of," Cassie said darkly. "But Mom hasn't exactly been super honest with us lately. Or ever, really."

That didn't seem totally fair, but I wasn't going to get into it with her right then. I just shrugged. "But how are you going to explain to Steve why you're asking?"

She bit her lip. "I'm not sure yet. We can just play it by ear, okay?" She looked around again. "But I think I'll text him to meet us around the corner from Viral Vinyl. We can sneak out of the store after we all get there. That place is so full of crazy nooks and crannies that the others won't even notice we're gone."

Just then Megan leaned across the aisle to say something to Cassie, and our conversation was over. It left me feeling uneasy. I'm not the type of person who just disobeys adults willy-nilly.

Still, it wasn't as if Cassie and I didn't know our way around San Antonio. And as Lavender had said, Viral Vinyl was just a few blocks from where we were supposed to be. We would be fine.

At least I hoped so.

4

CASSIE

I WANDERED ALONG at the back of the group as the tour guide led us from the courtyard into the shrine. This was the third time I'd been on a tour of the Alamo, so I wasn't exactly enthralled. Instead I was thinking about my plan. Steve had texted me back, promising to meet us near the record store. Now all Caitlyn and I had to do was get there ourselves.

Sneaking away from the River Walk wouldn't be too hard. We were allowed to wander through the entire huge pedestrian walkway, shopping and eating wherever we wanted. There were just a few rules: First, we had to stay in groups of at least two sets of partners. Second, we had to have at least one cell phone in each group. Third, we were supposed to use that cell phone to call a chaperone if we got lost or had any other trouble.

So, sneaking away to Viral Vinyl? Cake. But I was already a little worried about ditching my friends once we reached the record store. It was located in an old historic house, with three floors and tons of weird little rooms and hallways. How long would it take Megan and Lav—or Brayden—to notice I wasn't around? Then there was Cait. Her two geeky BFFs would probably tag along, and might actually notice when the third point in their nerd triangle went missing . . .

My gaze wandered toward the three of them. They were up near the front, seemingly fascinated by the guide's droning description of the history of Spanish missions in Texas. Or something like that; I wasn't really listening. Instead, I was wondering:

Could Caitlyn pull this off? Maybe I should have snuck away without her. My sister wasn't exactly stealthy when it came to this kind of thing, especially when Mom might catch her.

I glanced around, looking for Mom. But she was nowhere in sight. I turned, craning my neck to peer back toward the entrance.

"Everything all right, Miss Waters?" Principal Zale walked over to me.

"Sure." I forced a smile. "Um, have you seen my mother?"

The principal patted my arm. "She'll be back soon. She just slipped out to take care of some family business."

"Family business?" I echoed. "What do you mean?"

But Principal Zale was already hurrying forward, pointing sternly at Gabe Campbell, who was about to write on the stone walls with a pen. I followed. Family business? What was that all about?

As the tour guide moved on again, I pushed my way through the group until I reached my sister. I grabbed her by the arm, pulling her away from her nerd crew.

"Listen to this," I whispered. Then I told her what the principal had said about Mom.

Cait furrowed her brow. "Family business?" she said blankly. Then she gasped. "Wait! What if she's going to see Aunt Cheryl? Maybe this is it—my vision is about to come true!"

"Ssh!" I shot a look around, hoping nobody had heard her. The last thing we needed was to attract any extra check-out-the-crazy-twins attention. Especially from Gabe Campbell—he'd already overheard us talking about the Sight once, though we were pretty sure he didn't really believe anything we'd said.

"What should we do?" Caitlyn whispered, her brown eyes wide and worried.

I shrugged. "What *can* we do?" I whispered back. "I'm glad we're not meeting up with Steve at his house—just in case."

AN HOUR LATER, I was perched on a stool at a Tex-Mex place nibbling on a nacho. Caitlyn and I had chosen the place, since we were the only ones who'd been to the River Walk before. The food was good and cheap, and the service was fast—exactly what we were looking for.

Beside me, Lav and a couple of minions were arguing about their favorite bands or something. The B Boys were chowing down on their food, while Gabe Campbell sat scowling and picking at his quesadilla.

Oops. Gabe. I'd totally forgotten about him. He was partners with Brent, which meant he would have to be part of our plan. Would he go along with it, or would he rat us out to the chaperones?

I decided to let Brent worry about that. I had enough on my mind as it was.

For instance, Brayden. He'd already asked me if I'd help him find some moldy old blues album he wanted to buy his dad for Christmas. Sweet, right? But kind of inconvenient, since I was planning to bolt as soon as we got to Viral Vinyl . . .

"Hurry up and finish," Lavender ordered the B Boys loudly, breaking into my thoughts.

I glanced over and saw that Biff was still working his way through the four huge burritos he'd ordered.

Buzz grinned and leaned over to snatch one.

"Hey!" Biff said, his mouth full. "That's mine!"

"Eat faster, bro." Buzz shoved half the burrito into his mouth with one bite.

Meanwhile Lav turned to me with a frown. "So is your Goody Two-shoes sister actually coming with us?" she asked, obviously less than thrilled with the idea.

"Yeah, she's in." I picked one last cheese-drenched jalapeno off the nacho platter and popped it into my mouth. Mmm, spicy! Then I wiped my fingers on my napkin and got up.

Caitlyn and the rest of the Nerd Patrol were sitting a few tables away. As I approached, I could tell that they were actually talking about the history of the Alamo. Typical!

"You ready to fly?" I asked.

Caitlyn looked nervous. "I guess so." She glanced at her friends. "You're okay with this, right? Because if you're not, you don't have to come."

"Yeah." I agreed. Our group was already big enough to be less-than-stealthy. "You two could chill out here at the River Walk and cover for us."

"No, we want to come," Liam said. "Bianca thinks she might be able to find a copy of Blah-de-blah by Whoever at that record store."

Okay, that's not exactly what he said. But I kind of tuned out the names, since I'd never heard of the album or band he'd mentioned. No surprise there. Bianca plays the clarinet in the school band and isn't exactly cutting edge in her musical tastes.

"Whatever," I said. "Get ready, then, because we're leaving."

A few minutes later everyone was finally in motion. We'd lost some of the secondary minions, so only Abby and Emily were there, along with me, Megan, Lav, the B Boys, and the Nerd Patrol. Oh yeah, and Greasy Gabe Campbell. That brought the group total to thirteen people.

"Don't worry, Cass," Brent whispered when he saw me glaring at his partner, who was slouching along staring at Megan. "Gabe's not that bad, really. Anyway, I'll keep him in line."

"You'd better," I hissed. Then I glanced back to

make sure Brayden was keeping up on his crutches. He was swinging along, chatting and laughing with Liam. It still seemed weird that Cait's geekazoid friend had become actual buddies with the B Boys, but whatever.

"This way, everyone," Caitlyn called from the front of the group. "It's just a couple more blocks."

Viral Vinyl was tucked onto a quiet block just outside the artsy La Villita neighborhood. "Here we are," I said, gesturing to the bright yellow façade. There was no sign outside—just a big wooden record album hanging over the door.

"This is it?" Lavender sounded dubious. But Biff was already charging into the place, with Brent and the minions right behind him.

Gabe made a face. "I still can't believe we walked all this way for a stupid record store. Didn't any of you ever hear of downloading music?"

I rolled my eyes. The place was only a few blocks from the edge of the River Walk area. Maybe the cowboy boots Gabe always wore weren't made for walking, but that wasn't my problem.

"Come on, Gabe. It's an adventure!" Megan

actually smiled at the cretin. Then again, she's nice to everyone.

She followed the B Boys inside. Gabe shrugged and tagged along, and Lav hurried after them.

I hung back, waiting for the chance to make my escape. There was just one problem. My sister was heading inside, too, chattering with her friends about nerd music.

"Cait!" I hissed.

Caitlyn didn't hear me, but Brayden did. He'd started to follow the others, but now he paused and smiled at me. "Help me up the stairs, Cassie?"

I knew he probably didn't need my help—he'd gotten pretty handy with those crutches since the accident. But I knew flirting when I saw it.

"Sure, let's go." I tried not to blush as I put a hand on his elbow, helping him maneuver up the stairs into the store. Luckily no visions came. Because that was the last thing I needed right then.

Megan and the minions were just inside, digging through the bargain bin near the checkout. "Wow, this place is amazing!" Emily exclaimed, glancing around at the front room, which was crammed with boxes, bins, and shelves full of music in every format. Normally Viral Vinyl was one of my favorite places to browse, but today I barely spared it a second look.

"No kidding!" Lav raced over, clutching an album in both hands. "Check this out, guys—an autographed copy of Sakiko Star's first American EP!"

"Cool." I actually did think that was pretty cool. But I was way too distracted to think about Sakiko Star at the moment. "Hey, did you guys see where my sister went?"

"Um, I think she and her friends were heading upstairs?" Megan offered. Lav and the minions just shrugged.

I was charging toward the spiral staircase at the back of the shop when I heard my name. Oops. I'd almost forgotten about Brayden . . .

"Hey, should we check out the blues section first?" he asked. "I want to make sure I find that disc my dad wants."

"Oh." I forced a smile, doing my best to hide my impatience. "Sure! Let's go."

I could feel every second of the next fifteen minutes ticking past. Cousin Steve was always on time—it was a thing with him. Would Caitlyn and I be able to get out of here in time to meet him?

My phone buzzed in my pocket. "Oops, I guess I can turn my ringer back on," I said brightly, using that as an excuse to check out the text I'd just received.

Just as I'd thought—it was from Steve: *On my way, see you soon.*

That was a little weird. According to the time on my phone, we were supposed to meet Steve ten minutes ago. So maybe it was just as well that Caitlyn and I were running late, too.

But now we really needed to go. I glanced at Brayden, who was digging through some dusty albums. How was I going to make my getaway?

Amazingly, it was Caitlyn who came to the rescue. "Hey, guys!" she said cheerfully, hurrying toward us. "Brayden, do you mind if I steal our other trip buddy for a sec? I want to show her something."

"Sure, no prob." Luckily Brayden was distracted by peering at the labels on the albums in front of him. He didn't even look up as my sister and I headed toward the entrance.

There was just one more problem: Greasy Gabe.

He was lounging by the bargain bin, looking bored.

"Where are you going?" he asked when he saw Cait and me coming.

A quick glance at Caitlyn showed her looking like a bunny in headlights. Okay, it was going to be up to me to come to the rescue this time.

I thought fast. "Uh, Cait's having an allergy attack," I told Gabe. "We're just going out for some fresh air."

"Yeah." Caitlyn let out a loud, dramatic sniffle. "Uh, dust."

"Better stay back," I advised Gabe. "When she sneezes, anyone nearby needs a raincoat!"

"Gross." Gabe shot us a disgusted look, then turned and wandered off toward the heavy metal section.

"Whew!" I said under my breath. "Come on, let's book before someone else tries to stop us."

This time we actually made it outside. "We'd better hurry," Cait said. "Steve's probably waiting."

"He's late, too—didn't you see his text?" When Caitlyn reached for her phone, I yanked her along the sidewalk. "Never mind—let's just get there."

I'd arranged to meet Steve at the nearest bus stop. He was already there, perched on the bench, when we turned the corner.

"Steve!" I smiled, realizing how weird it was that we hadn't seen him in weeks.

"Twin dorks!" he exclaimed, rushing to meet us.

But his smile looked a little strained. "What's wrong?" Caitlyn asked after hugging him. "You look weird."

"Gee, thanks." He rolled his eyes. But then his gaze darted around, as if he was looking for something. Or someone. "Look, let's get off the street, okay?"

"Sure. Why?" I asked.

He glanced around again. "It's possible I'm being followed," he hissed.

"Followed?" Caitlyn's eyes widened. "What do you mean?"

He just shook his head and gestured toward a nearby café. "Just come on," he said. "We seriously need to talk."

5
CAITLYN

SEEING STEVE WAS amazing. He looked just like he always did—a little taller than us, with a short Afro and a dimple in one cheek. But he was definitely acting weird. He practically dragged Cassie and me into some overpriced tourist café. We grabbed seats in the back and told the waitress we only wanted sodas. She seemed a little annoyed, but the place wasn't crowded, so she shrugged and hurried off.

"Okay, spill," Cassie ordered as soon as we were alone. "Who's following you, James Bond, Junior?"

Steve stuck out his tongue at her. "I'm serious. Listen, I should start at the beginning."

"Okay," I said. "By the way, did our mom show up at your house today, by any chance?"

Steve held up his hand. "Enough with the grilling, twin dorks," he said. "Just let me tell the story, okay? Because I think you're really going to want to hear it."

I shot my sister an amused look. Typical Steve! Just because he was a year older, he'd always tried to boss us around. But with two against one, it didn't usually work.

Cassie didn't meet my eye. She was leaning across the table, staring at Steve. "Okay, so tell it already," she said. "We're listening."

Just then the waitress bustled back over. She plunked down three sodas, sloshing half of them onto the table. "Thanks," I said, but the waitress was already racing off again.

Good. Because I was really curious now.

"Okay," Steve said. "So it started the other day—"

"When?" Cassie broke in.

"I dunno." Steve shrugged. "Monday, I think? Anyway, I was fixing myself a snack after school when someone rang the doorbell. I answered, and it was some skeevy-looking dude."

"What do you mean, skeevy?" I asked.

He shrugged again. "I mean, he looked normal enough at first. Just some white guy in jeans and a dark sweatshirt. But he seemed twitchy, sort of shifty looking, you know?"

"Okay," Cassie said.

"So he said he was looking for D. Waters." Steve shot us each a meaningful look. "D. Waters? Get it?"

I blinked. "But there's no D. Waters at your house," I said. "Just C. Waters-Wiley—Aunt Cheryl, that is—and then you and Uncle Charles. Both Wileys."

"There's a D. Waters at our house, though." Cassie shot me a duh-catch-up-already look. "Mom. D. Waters—Deidre Waters."

"Right. But I wasn't really thinking about that at the time," Steve said. "Because this guy said he had something very important to give to D. Waters, and that he'd been assured by his . . ." He paused, squinting at his soda glass. "Uh, I think he called it his 'esteemed photographer friend' or something like that? Anyway, he said he'd been assured by someone that there would be a big reward if he delivered this important thing."

"What thing?" Cassie was starting to look confused.

I knew how she felt. "And why was he looking for Mom at your house?"

Steve sipped his drink. "I didn't see what the thing was at first. He had it in his pocket, I guessed— at least, he kept sticking his hand in there. Anyway, around then, my mom heard us talking and came out to see what was up."

"Did she know the guy?" I asked.

"No. He said the same thing to her as he'd said to me, and then mentioned that he'd already been to 'the place over on Refugio Street.'"

I gasped. "That's our old address!"

"Exactly." Steve nodded. "I guess when he didn't find Aunt Deidre there, he searched for the name Waters and found my mom."

I nodded. Aunt Cheryl had hyphenated her last

name, and Waters came first. "So did you guys tell him she'd moved away?"

"Yeah, my mom explained the whole deal. And he practically freaked out." Steve played with his straw. "He started blabbing about how he didn't have time to go all the way out to Aura, and that someone was already on to him—"

"On to him?" Cassie blinked. "What's that mean?"

"You got me," Steve said. "Anyway, my mom was obviously pretty suspicious of the whole deal. She tried to send him away, but he kept insisting he had to hand over whatever it was to her, since she was D. Waters's sister. Finally, he actually pulled the thing out."

"So what was it?" Cassie asked.

Steve shrugged. "Just some cheap souvenir key ring," he said. "Shaped like the British flag, all chipped up and old looking. Totally random, right? Only when Mom got a look at it, she flipped out. She grabbed the thing, threw some money at the guy, and rushed upstairs and locked herself in her room."

I did my best to take that in. Aunt Cheryl was more laid-back than Mom, but almost as sensible. No way would she fall for some con man's trick to get money out of her.

Cassie looked perplexed, too. "Wait," she said. "There must have been more to it. It was really just a key ring?"

"Yeah, and a note." Steve fiddled with his straw again. "It had your old address on it, and something about a reward—I didn't get a good look. Oh! And I think there were some words scratched on the back of the key ring—the guy pointed that out to Mom. But I didn't see what it said."

My sister and I traded a look. "You said this happened this past Monday, right?" Cassie said slowly.

I gasped as my twintuition told me what she was thinking about—that phone call from Aunt Cheryl on Monday afternoon. "So that's why she was calling," I exclaimed. "She was telling Mom about the key ring."

"But why was she so freaked out?" Cassie wrapped both hands around her soda glass. "Could it have to do with, um . . ." Her voice trailed off and she stared at me.

"What?" Steve looked from her to me and back again. "Hey, what aren't you guys telling me? Spill!"

"It's nothing," Cass said quickly. "We just, um . . ."

"Eh, eh, eh!" Steve waggled his finger in our faces. "You know I can read you guys like a book. What's going on?"

"It's about our dad," I blurted out. "We think he might still be alive!"

Steve sat back. "What? But he died, like, a million years ago."

"More like ten and a half," Cassie corrected. "But yeah, we thought so, too. Only our grandmother just showed up—"

"Maw Maw Jean?" Steve said.

"No—our other grandmother." I bit my lip. "Our dad's mom."

"She's British," Cassie added.

"Oh, right. That's where they met, right? In England?" Steve said. "Mom told me he was a local civilian who worked on the military base where she was stationed, or something like that."

"Yeah, something like that." I felt a little weirded out all of a sudden. Until very recently, our mom had refused to tell us anything about our dad at all. Just that he'd been white, and they'd met when she was stationed in England. Now it sounded as if Steve had known more than us all along. At least a little.

"So she just showed up and said he was alive?" Steve prompted.

I kicked at the metal leg of the table. "Sort of . . ."

Once again, Cassie and I exchanged a long look. We'd grown up with Steve, and he knew everything about us. Except for one pretty major new thing.

Up until now, we hadn't told anyone about the Sight—at least not anyone who hadn't already known about it. In other words, Grandmother Lockwood and Mom.

Steve was watching us through narrowed eyes. "You guys are terrible at keeping secrets," he said. "So whatever you're making moony eyes at each other about, you might as well just tell me. Because you know I'll get it out of you sooner or later."

"He's right," Cass told me. "Anyway, we can trust him."

She had a point. Steve hadn't told anyone about the time Cassie had snuck out to go to a concert last year. Or about my big crush on the handyman who'd painted our apartment. This secret was bigger than those, but I knew he wouldn't give it away. But would he believe us? That was a whole separate question.

"Okay," I said, taking a deep breath. "It's a good thing you're already sitting down, because you're not going to believe this . . ."

Taking turns, Cassie and I told him about the Sight. The basics, anyway. Our weird, confusing visions. The day we'd realized we were both having them, and that they were showing us the future. And finally, Grandmother Lockwood's explanation about how one person in every generation of our family inherited the same special power. Only with us, it had turned out to be two people—twins.

Steve didn't say anything while we talked, mostly just sipped his soda and tapped his fingers on the table. When we finished, he looked kind of confused.

"This is a joke, right?" he said. "I mean, seriously—my twin-dork cousins don't really have superpowers. No way."

"Want to bet?" Cassie shot me a look, then reached over and grabbed his hand. Then she frowned. "Hmm. Nothing."

"What are you doing?" Steve yanked his hand away. "Seriously, what's the punch line, guys?"

I guessed that Cass had hoped to prove what we were saying with a vision about Steve. The trouble is, the Sight doesn't work that way. The visions come whenever they come. We've got no control over them.

Still, I figured it was worth a shot . . . Reaching over the table, I grabbed Steve by the wrist. Then I gasped as the vision hit me . . .

My cousin faded away, replaced by a brighter, sharper Steve . . .

By the time Steve jerked his arm away, I was smiling. "What?" Cassie demanded. "Did you have one?"

"Uh-huh." I took a deep breath, doing my best to

banish the spacey feeling leftover from the vision. Then I raised my eyebrows at Steve. "Do you have a dentist appointment coming up soon?"

"Next week—why?" Steve looked startled.

"Because I saw you in the chair." I smirked. "Looking terrified while the dentist was pointing at your X-ray."

"Uh-oh, someone's got a cavity!" Cassie teased.

Steve scowled at us. "Shut up. You're just messing with me, right?"

"Nope. But hey, it looks like you switched from Dr. Chan's office," I said. "Your dentist now is an older guy with a mustache, right?"

Steve looked startled. "How did you—wait. Are you guys for real about this?"

"For real, for real," I assured him, while Cassie nodded.

He pushed his soda away. "You didn't just ask my mom who my dentist is now or something? Just as a joke, or whatever?"

"Why would we do that?" Cassie rolled her eyes. "Talk about a lame joke."

Just then my phone pinged. It was a text from Liam wondering where I was. "Oops," I said. "Look, we don't have a ton of time. And we need to talk about this key chain thing."

I quickly texted Liam back, saying I was in the bathroom and would find him and Bianca soon. Meanwhile Cassie was asking Steve to tell us again exactly what had happened on Monday afternoon, every detail.

"So do you know what that key ring could be?" he finished. "Why did my mom freak out about it?"

"I'm not sure." Cass drummed on the table with her fingernails. "But Mom met our dad in England, right? Could the British flag have something to do with that?"

"I wonder what it says on the back." I tucked my phone in my pocket. "I wish you'd gotten a better look."

"I can try to find it," Steve offered.

"Thanks," Cassie said. "But Mom snuck away from the group while we were touring the Alamo earlier. She told one of the other chaperones she had to take care of some family business."

"I bet she's over at Aunt Cheryl's right now," I finished. "Actually, I'm sure of it—because I already saw her there."

"Huh?" Steve blinked at me. "What do you mean? You were at my house?"

"Keep up, genius," Cassie told him. "She saw it in a vision."

"Really?" He sat up straight. "What do you mean?"

I filled him in on the vision I'd had of Mom and Aunt Cheryl staring at something—that flag key ring, I realized now—in Aunt Cheryl's hallway. Steve looked impressed.

"Whoa, so this Sight thing is pretty crazy!" he exclaimed.

"Tell us about it," Cassie said.

"Okay. But this makes it easier, right?" Steve shrugged. "Aunt Deidre might still be at my house now. So, I'll just go home and ask her what's up."

Cassie and I traded a look. "Have you *met* our mother?" Cass exclaimed. "Because if she doesn't want to tell you, you know she's not going to tell you."

I nodded. "And based on how she's been acting about all this, I'm guessing she's not going to tell you. Or us." I sighed. "So what should we do?"

Just then a snippet of a Sakiko Star song rang out from Cassie's purse. She grabbed her phone and checked it.

"Uh-oh, that's Megan," she said. "She wants to know where I am. With, like, four question marks at the end."

A glance at the clock on the café wall showed that we'd been away from our friends for quite a while. "We should probably get back before they get suspicious," I said. "But I really want to keep talking about this!"

"Yeah." Cassie stared at Steve. "But hey, maybe we can tell our friends the truth—at least part of it."

"What do you mean?" Steve sucked up the last of his soda.

"We can tell them we snuck off to meet you," Cassie explained, pointing to Steve. "I mean, you're

our cousin, and we're practically right in your neighborhood. Makes sense, right?"

"Sure," Steve agreed. "Then I can hang with you
guys, and maybe we can find time to talk more."

I smiled. "Sounds like a plan. Now come on, let's
get back to Viral Vinyl."

It was only a five-minute walk to the record
store. We practiced our alibi on the way.

Megan was waiting at the door, her face paler
than usual. "Oh, thank goodness!" she blurted out.
"Is Lav with you?"

"Lav?" Cassie echoed. "No, Cait and I just slipped
out to meet up with our cousin. This is Steve, he
lives right down the—"

Abby and Emily appeared behind her, looking
frantic. "Did you find them?" Abby cried.

"The twins are here," Megan shouted. "But they
haven't seen Lav either!"

"Oh, man," Emily moaned. "This is what I was
afraid of when I saw her with that guy . . ."

"Wait." I held up both hands. "Slow down, people. What guy? What's going on?"

Megan took a deep breath. "Ems saw Lav flirting with a cute guy earlier."

"Really cute, and just Lav's type," Abby confirmed. "I saw him, too. He looked around eighteen, maybe? Dark hair, really well dressed."

"Okay." So far, I wasn't seeing the problem here. I didn't spend much time with Lavender, but even I knew that she flirted with anything in pants.

"Yeah," Emily went on. "I saw them heading for the exit twenty minutes ago."

Megan nodded grimly. "And nobody has seen Lavender since."

6

CASSIE

"WAIT." I COULD tell my friends were panicking, but I wasn't ready to join them just yet. "Did you trying calling Lav? She has her phone with her today, right?"

Megan nodded. "I left, like, five voice messages, and I texted her a few times, too."

"Me, too," the minions chorused.

I gulped. Okay, time to panic now. Lavender was obsessed with her phone. She was famous for responding to texts within seconds. Split seconds, even.

Just then Biff and Buzz barged out of the store. "Did you find her?" Buzz demanded.

"No, just the twins." Abby glared at Cait and me as if we were to blame for Lav's disappearance. "Lav wasn't with them."

"Oh, man." Biff glanced at Steve. "Hey. Who's this?"

We quickly introduced our cousin and explained about sneaking out to meet him. It was the easiest cover story ever to pull off. None of our friends paid much attention aside from tossing Steve a couple of polite "heys."

"Let's get the others," Megan said. "We need to figure out what to do."

She rushed inside, followed by the guys and the minions. But Caitlyn held me and Steve back. She looked freaked-out.

"What if this is our fault?" she hissed.

"Huh?" I shook my head. "Come on, Cait. "We didn't kidnap Lav."

"No. But we came on this trip, even though Grandmother Lockwood said it could be"— Caitlyn gulped—"dangerous. Plus, we both had weird visions about Lavender."

A shiver ran through me as I realized she was right. We'd both had confusing visions recently featuring Lav—visions that might be coming true right now. Plus, we'd been warned not to come on this trip. And we already knew some crazy stuff was going on—Steve had mentioned that the guy who'd brought the key ring had said that someone was after him. And Steve himself had worried that someone might be following him just now. What if . . . ?

"Never mind," I blurted out, cutting off the thought before I could finish. "Let's just go in and see what's up."

We hurried inside. The rest of the group was huddled in the back of the store near the hip-hop section. Caitlyn's friends were there, too. Greasy Gabe was hanging back a little from the rest, leaning against a bin of old CDs, looking bored.

"We've got to call the chaperones," Megan was saying when we joined them. "If Lav's in trouble . . ."

"But what if she just went off to, like, flirt with that guy or whatever, and she comes back soon?"

Brent said. "She might not be in trouble at all. But we'll all be in big trouble if we tell the chaperones we snuck away."

Megan shrugged. "Lav's safety is more important than us not getting in trouble."

"Yeah, duh," Abby added. "Don't you even care about Lav at all?"

"No," Gabe spoke up with a smirk.

"Zip it, bro," Biff told him. "This is serious."

Everyone started talking at once, arguing one way or the other. Most of the group was ready to call the principal, or maybe the police. Only Brent and Buzz seemed to think we should keep looking for Lav ourselves. Oh, and Greasy Gabe seemed willing to just let her stay lost. Nice, right?

But I was hardly listening. Caitlyn's comment had reminded me about those visions. Could there be a clue in one of them?

I ran through the visions in my head. There had been a total of four featuring Lavender. First Cait had seen Lav kissing Biff on a darkened bus. That one was probably going to play out a little later, on the trip home.

But it might not happen at all if we don't find her, I reminded myself.

The visions could be a little confusing that way. Sometimes we saw visions of events that never occurred, because we managed to change them before they happened. But I didn't feel like getting my brain all tangled up thinking about that right now, so I returned to my list of Lav visions.

The second one had been Cait's, too. In that one, she'd seen Lav getting dragged by the wrist down a city sidewalk, looking annoyed.

Finally there had been mine. I'd actually had the first one when I'd been touching my sister, but Lav had been in the vision, too. I'd seen her and Cait standing in a brightly lit shop with posters of ladies with crazy and colorful hairdos on the walls. It hadn't lasted long—just long enough for me to watch Lav toss a magazine at Cait.

Then there was the one from earlier this week when we were shopping. In that one I'd seen some-one grabbing a screaming Lav's phone and smashing it, then shoving her through a darkened doorway.

Closing my eyes, I thought over the visions again.

There had to be a clue in them somewhere! I tried to remember everything Caitlyn had told me about hers. She'd said the background had looked like a city—maybe right here in San Antonio? She hadn't been sure, though she'd mentioned seeing signs in Spanish . . .

Could that be a clue? My head started pounding as an idea popped into my mind . . .

"No, Megan is right," Caitlyn was saying, while most of the others nodded in agreement. "We're wasting time arguing about this. Let's call my mom, and she can get in touch with the police . . ."

"Wait," I blurted out. "I just thought of something."

Suddenly all eyes were on me. "What is it, Cassie?" Megan asked.

"Um, Steve might have seen Lav on his way to meet us." I widened my eyes briefly at my cousin, hoping he'd play along. "He told us about this girl who looked like Lav. She was, um, being dragged along by the wrist by some cute older guy."

I put a little extra emphasis on the words "dragged along by the wrist." Caitlyn actually got it right away—I saw her let out a little gasp, though I was pretty sure nobody else noticed.

"Huh?" Brent looked confused. "Wait, how does your cousin know Lav?"

"He doesn't," I said. "But I sent him a picture of us once, and, well . . ."

"Yeah, um, that's right." Steve was always a pretty quick study. "I'm not sure it was her, but maybe . . ."

"Anyway," I continued quickly, "he was passing by El Mercado when he saw her. So maybe we should check there before we call anyone."

This time Cait's gasp was a little louder, and I knew she'd just caught up for real. "Right!" she blurted out. "We should totally check there."

"Wait, what's El Mercado?" Buzz asked.

"It's the largest Mexican market in the United States," Liam said. Leave it to nerd-boy to play a walking wiki.

"Dude, let's go," Biff said. "I can totally translate!"

I rolled my eyes. Biff's mom was Mexican-American, but if he actually spoke Spanish, it was news to me.

"Just come on," I told the whole group. "It's not far from here."

We raced out of the record store. "Lead the way, okay?" I whispered to Steve. "I need to talk to Cait."

"This way, folks!" he called out. "Follow the local boy."

As the others charged down the sidewalk after my cousin, I grabbed Caitlyn and held her back. We followed along a few paces behind the group.

"You're thinking about my vision, right?" she whispered. "Do you think it was a clue that we might find Lavender at El Mercado?"

"You tell me. You're the one who saw it."

She shrugged. "I guess it could be. I mean, there were signs in Spanish and English. But I didn't see any of those flag decorations they have there, or any touristy-looking stalls, either."

"The whole place isn't like that," I reminded her. "Anyway, there are some businesses nearby that could be what you saw, too."

"But maybe that guy just dragged her through El Mercado on his way somewhere else," Caitlyn said.

I frowned at her. "I thought you were supposed to be Miss Optimistic," I said. "Let's just see what we can find, okay? Keep a lookout for anything you saw in your v—"

Caitlyn cut me off with an elbow to the ribs. Brayden had stopped, and we were about to catch up with him.

"You okay?" I asked him.

"Yeah," he said. "Just having trouble going so fast on these stupid crutches."

By then the other B Boys had noticed he'd stopped. They hurried toward us.

"We'll help you, bro," Buzz offered. "Cassie'll carry your crutches. Right, Cass?"

"Sure." I reached out.

As Brayden handed over the crutches, I froze. It was a vision—just a short one, since our hands only touched for a second. All I saw was Minion Emily shoving Brayden, looking angry.

Luckily the boys didn't notice. Brayden was slinging his arms over Brent's and Buzz's shoulders. The two of them hoisted him up, carrying him between them with his cast skimming the sidewalk.

"Let me know when you get tired and I'll jump in," Biff offered as they all took off after the others.

"What was that?" Caitlyn whispered, shooting me a look of concern.

"Vision," I replied. "Nothing to do with Lav. Ems was in it, and she was wearing something totally different from her outfit today."

My sister smiled. "I guess sometimes your fashion obsession actually comes in handy." Her smile faded as she glanced at the others, who were almost at the next intersection. "Come on, let's catch up."

7
CAITLYN

IT TOOK US maybe twenty minutes to reach El Mercado. Even on a weekday, plenty of tourists were wandering around. We stopped in the middle of the pedestrian walkway near a stand full of brightly painted vases and baskets.

"Okay, where'd you see this guy?" Megan asked Steve breathlessly.

Steve shot Cassie and me a panicked look. "Um, I don't remember," he mumbled.

"What?" Abby scowled at him. "Well, you'd better

remember! Because Lav's life could depend on it!"

"Freaking out isn't going to help, Abby," Cassie told her friend, raising her voice a little to be heard over the Latin music playing nearby. "Let's just look around, okay? What did the guy you saw with Lav look like again?"

"Dark hair, medium height," Abby said. "A really adorable smile."

"Don't call him adorable," Emily chided her. "He might be a horrible kidnapper!"

"I know, I'm just describing him," Abby whined. "I think he was wearing jeans and a jacket?"

"He was," Emily confirmed. "It looked like linen."

"What color?" Cassie asked.

"Dark blue, I think?"

"It looked gray to me," Abby put in.

Just then four or five little kids raced into view, shrieking and waving their arms. A man was chasing after them with an ice cream cone in one hand and a cell phone in the other. "No running, y'all!" he hollered. "Wait for me!"

"Watch it!" Biff exclaimed as a kid bounced off

him, almost crashing into Brayden before skittering on out of sight with the rest of his group right behind him.

"Better take these back now." Cassie handed the crutches to Brayden, who'd been leaning against a railing.

"Thanks." Brayden tucked the crutches into place under his arms. "Should we split up and look around for Lav and this guy?"

"No!" Emily blurted out. "I mean, I don't think we should split up. We can search together, right?"

The others agreed. I was glad. We were in enough trouble as it was without half the group getting lost.

We started walking, peering into each shop or restaurant we passed. I was checking an art stall when Steve caught up to me.

"So is this wild goose chase about one of your vision thingies?" he whispered.

"Ssh!" I glanced around to make sure nobody was close enough to hear. Luckily the music was still playing, making it a little easier to talk without being overheard. "Yeah, I saw Lavender in a vision getting dragged along through the city. We think it might be around here, since there were some Spanish signs and stuff in the background."

Steve looked a little confused. "Wait. I thought you guys said all of Cait's visions show good things happening. If someone was going to see this girl getting kidnapped, wouldn't it be Cass?"

I hadn't really thought about that. Cassie was always going on about how I got to see the good stuff while she got stuck with the bad. "You'd think so, right?" I replied slowly. "But sometimes the visions can be pretty confusing. Like, once I saw Liam all bloody and thought the B Boys were beating him up or something."

"B Boys?" Steve echoed.

"That's what we call those guys." I waved a hand toward Brayden and his friends, who were a few yards ahead of us. "Anyway, the vision turned out to show the guys helping Liam after he fell and hurt himself. That's how he became friends with them."

"I get it." Steve nodded, looking thoughtful. "So it looked bad, but it turned out to show something that was mostly good."

I smiled, realizing how much I'd missed having

my cousin around. "I'm glad we told you about the visions," I said. "It feels good to talk about them with someone other than Grandmother Lockwood."

Before Steve could reply, Gabe let out a shout. "I see her!" he exclaimed, waving from the entrance to a market stall a little way ahead.

We all raced toward him. Brayden was in such a hurry that he caught one of his crutches on a loose brick in the walkway and almost fell.

When we reached the stall, which held all kinds of Mexican crafts, Gabe was grinning. Then he waved a hand toward a witch-shaped piñata hanging from the ceiling.

"See? Lav's looking better than usual, right?" he said.

Megan and Emily groaned. "Gabe, you jerk!" Abby yelled.

"Not funny, dude." Biff gave Gabe a punch on the arm that looked a little too hard to be totally playful.

"Ow." Gabe stepped away, rubbing his arm. "Look, this is stupid. Let's just call the cops already."

I was starting to agree. El Mercado only covered about three city blocks. But it was feeling way bigger right now. Besides, we didn't even know for sure that this was where my vision had taken place. There could be lots of other places in the city with signs in Spanish.

But Cassie was already shaking her head. "We've got to find her," she said. "Come on, just keep looking."

She hurried forward, scattering a small flock of pigeons as she went. The rest of us followed.

I was peering into a restaurant lobby when Bianca caught up to me. She looked slightly puzzled.

"Hey, I thought you said your relatives live in King William," she said. "Isn't that neighborhood south of the River Walk?"

"More or less, yeah," I said. "Why?"

"So how did your cousin see Lavender here in El Mercado on his way to meet you?" Bianca waved a hand at the colorful market around us. "According to the map I looked at before the trip, we're pretty much west of the River Walk now. Nowhere near Steve's house, right?"

I gulped. Normally I adored Bianca's logical mind. Right now? Not so much.

"Um, I guess he must have gone somewhere right after school?" I forced what I hoped was a carefree little laugh. "Anyway, I'm glad he came past here. It could be our best chance to find Lavender, right?"

"Sure, I guess." Bianca still looked troubled.

But before she could say anything else, a group of tourists came pouring out of the restaurant. They were all chattering away in what sounded like some kind of eastern European language. Bianca and I ended up being swept out along with them, and I took the opportunity to dart away to join Steve again.

"Whew!" I shot a look behind me, making sure that Bianca hadn't followed me. "I think some of the other kids are getting a little suspicious of our story."

"Really?" Steve looked worried. "Maybe we should—hey! That's the guy!"

His shout attracted the attention of the others. Abby gasped when she looked where Steve was pointing.

"Yeah, that's him!" she shrieked. "That's the guy who took Lav!"

They were looking at a handsome guy in his late teens or early twenties. He'd been leaning against a wall staring at his cell phone, but when he heard the shouts, he turned and squinted at us.

"How'd you recognize him?" I asked Steve, a little freaked-out that our cover story seemed to be coming true.

"That's the guy I saw following me earlier," he said. "Remember? I spotted him a couple of times on my way to meet you."

We followed the others, who were charging toward the guy in a group. Maybe that wasn't the smartest thing to do, but there was no stopping Megan and her friends. Besides, we were in a public place, so I figured we would probably be safe. Already, some tourists and vendors were peering over curiously.

"What did you do with her?" Megan demanded, hands on her hips.

The guy looked startled for a second. Then he smirked.

"Oh, wait," he said. "Are you the rich girl's friends?

How'd you find me?" Then he waved a hand. "Never mind, I don't care. Go away."

He started to turn away, but Abby grabbed his sleeve. "Stop!" she ordered. "Where's Lav? What'd you do with her?"

The man rolled his eyes. "Settle down, kids," he said. "Your friend is fine." He smirked again. "Come to think of it, what's it worth to you to find her?"

"Huh?" Emily said blankly.

"What's it worth?" The guy rubbed his fingers together. "You want me to tell you where she is, right? So make it worth my while."

"I'll worth your while, dude," Biff growled, taking a quick step forward. Buzz and Brent were right behind him, looking aggressive.

Uh-oh. Things were feeling pretty tense. I guessed that Liam thought so, too, since I noticed him sidling toward the back of the group.

"Don't touch me, boys," the guy snarled, taking a step back from the football players. "Otherwise you'll never see your whiny little friend again."

Megan gasped. "Guys, stop!" she begged.

Bianca stepped forward. "Calm down," she told the B Boys sharply. "Let me talk to him."

I traded a surprised look with Cassie. Bianca was normally pretty quiet. She barely ever spoke up in class, even though she always knew most of the answers.

Nobody said anything as Bianca turned to face the older guy. "What do you want?" she asked.

"What do you think?" he said with a sneer. "Money. How much you got?"

"We're not giving you anything," Abby cried. "We'll call the cops!"

"Go ahead." The guy shrugged. "I'll be long gone by the time they show up. And then how will you ever find your little friend?"

I looked around, hoping someone would come over and intervene. But the Latin music was too loud for our voices to carry far. Most of the bystanders had already wandered off or gone back to what they were doing.

Meanwhile the guy crossed his arms over his chest. "I should probably just steal her fancy jewelry and credit cards and be done with it."

"No!" Megan blurted out. "Come on, guys—how much cash do y'all have on you?"

"Give us a second," Bianca told the guy in a calm voice. "We'll see what we can do."

I stared at her, impressed by the way she was keeping her cool. When she looked at me, I stuck my hand in my pocket. "Um, I've got a twenty and a few ones," I offered.

Everyone else was digging in their purses and pockets, too. Well, almost everyone. Liam had disappeared. I couldn't help being a little disappointed in him. He might be a little bit nerdy, but I'd never thought he was a coward.

Then there was Gabe. When Bianca looked at him, he shrugged and tossed her a penny.

"There. That's what that girl's worth to me," he drawled.

That actually made the creep laugh. "Okay, what's the total?" he asked.

"Um . . ." Bianca counted the bills in her hand. "One hundred and fourteen dollars?"

The guy let out a snort. "Are you kidding? I thought you kids were rich. I'll need at least a thousand."

"But we don't have that much!" Emily cried.

He shrugged. "So get it. Kids like you must have ATM cards, right? Like I said, you gotta make it worth my while." He frowned slightly as he turned away. "Maybe that'll make up for getting here too late to grab back that tacky old key chain . . . ," he muttered under his breath.

My eyes widened. I glanced at Cassie. "Did you hear that?" I hissed.

She stared back at me. I could practically see the wheels turning in her brain. They were turning in mine, too. Suddenly this was all making a little more sense. Steve had seen that guy following him—what if he'd followed him all the way from Aunt Cheryl's house? What if he'd figured out that the kids in the record store were with us, and decided to pick Lavender's brain to figure out how to get at us—and maybe get his hands on that key ring? Obviously someone thought it was pretty important . . .

"What's all this then?" a voice boomed out.

We all spun around. A pair of uniformed San Antonio police officers were standing there behind us—with Liam right next to them!

I smiled, quickly sending a mental apology to Liam. He wasn't a coward after all. He'd gone for help while the guy was distracted by the rest of us!

"He kidnapped our friend!" Abby yelled, pointing at the guy.

The guy looked startled. But he reacted quickly, taking off at a sprint. There was a wall behind him, so he darted out and around to one side.

Oh, no! The police officers were on the other side of the group. They'd never be able to grab him before he got away!

"Stop!" Brayden yelled. He leaped forward as if he planned to tackle the bad guy. But I could already see that he was too far away . . .

"Oof!" the kidnapper grunted as Brayden flung one of his crutches forward—catching the guy right in the knees!

The bad guy went sprawling to the sidewalk.

So did Brayden, as the toss threw him off-balance. I gasped as I saw the vision I'd had earlier coming true—Brayden flat out on the bricks with his crutches just out of reach . . .

But I didn't have much time to focus on that. The police officers were already hurrying forward; the male cop had a pair of handcuffs in one hand, while his female partner had her hand on the grip of her baton. Liam was keeping pace with them, chattering excitedly at them about Lavender and the rest.

"Hold still, sir," the male cop said as he grabbed the bad guy and hauled him to his feet. "You have the right to remain silent . . ."

8
CASSIE

THE BAD GUY might have been cute, but he was pretty much a jerk. He refused to tell the cops where Lav was unless they let him go. And I'd spent enough time living with a cop—aka Officer Mom—to know that wasn't going to happen.

"Don't worry, kids," the female officer told us as her partner wrestled the handcuffed guy toward the street. "We'll get him to talk."

I traded a worried look with Caitlyn. Our visions had gotten us this far, but now what?

Just then a second pair of officers arrived. "What's going on? You need backup?" one of them asked.

"It's under control." The female officer nodded toward the perp. "Maybe you can help these kids get back where they belong." She glanced at Liam. "Apparently they wandered off from their school group at the River Walk."

Oh, great. Nerd-boy might have helped collar the kidnapper, but did he have to rat us out at the same time?

But whatever. I wasn't looking forward to the long walk back anyway.

"Actually, could you take the three of us to our cousin's house?" Caitlyn spoke up. She gestured toward Steve. "He lives in King William. And our mom is probably there, too—she's a chaperone."

The cop looked surprised. "I don't know. I'll need to talk to an adult before I leave you kids anywhere."

"Wait, we're not going back without you," Abby spoke up.

"Yeah. Safety in numbers, right?" Buzz shrugged.

"Principal Zale can't kill all of us at once."

I gritted my teeth. Caitlyn and I really needed to talk to Mom about this whole key ring thing. And we wouldn't be able to do that with half the sixth grade hanging around.

"It's okay, just go back to the group," I told my friends. "We'll be there soon."

"No way." Brayden was back on his feet by now, only a little scuffed up. "We should all stay together."

"It's okay," Caitlyn told me. "We can all go. It's fine."

I wasn't so sure. But what choice did we have?

Steve pulled out his cell phone. "I'll call my mom."

It took a couple more police cars, but we all ended up getting shuttled down to Steve's house. His family lived in a cute yellow Craftsman cottage on a quiet street. I actually felt a little choked up when I saw it. How many times had I eaten dinner in the oak-floored dining room there over the past few years? How many holidays and Sunday afternoons had I spent in the cozy front room with my family? I couldn't even count.

All of that flew out of my mind as soon as I got a load of Mom's face. Category ten hurricane.

Aunt Cheryl emerged from the house right behind Mom. Steve must have explained the whole deal to her on the phone, because she invited everyone in for sweet tea and cookies. The cops said no thanks, since they were on duty. But soon everyone else was sitting around in the front room chattering about what had just happened.

Mom, Cait, and Steve helped Aunt Cheryl pass out glasses of tea, while I fetched some Band-Aids and helped Brayden patch up a couple of scrapes on his arms and legs. What can I say? I'm all about helping people. Especially cute people with amazing brown eyes . . .

As Mom handed Liam the last glass, she cleared her throat. "I've already called Principal Zale and let him know where you are," she said. "Ms. Church is on her way down here to help me get you all back to the buses."

Brent groaned. "Are we in trouble?"

"What do you think?" Mom retorted.

Yikes. She sounded pretty riled up. Caitlyn and I called that her scarymama voice.

Aunt Cheryl cleared her throat. "Cassie, Caitlyn, Deidre, come on with me now," she said. "Let's see if we can dig up some more cookies for your friends, all right?"

She waggled her eyebrows at us meaningfully. I hopped to my feet.

Steve must have caught his mother's look, too. "I'll help," he said, following the rest of us into the kitchen.

"No need, son," Aunt Cheryl said. "You stay back and entertain our guests."

"It's okay." Cait glanced over her shoulder at the front room, then lowered her voice. "He knows."

Aunt Cheryl looked surprised. "Oh?"

"Yeah," Steve told her. "The twins told me all about—you know."

"Let's get out of earshot," Mom said, heading for the back hall.

Soon we were all shut into the spare bedroom. Steve and I collapsed into the two chairs in there. Aunt Cheryl and Caitlyn perched on the edge of the bed, while Mom paced around like a caged tiger. Only scarier. I didn't even want to think about how long Cait and I were going to be grounded for this whole stunt . . .

"All right, what's this about Lavender?" Mom demanded. "What happened to her?"

"We're not sure," Caitlyn said. "Cassie and I were off talking to Steve, and when we got back, the others said she went off with some guy."

"Oh, Lordy." Aunt Cheryl shook her head. "The boy craziness starts earlier and earlier all the time. It won't be long until you have two full-fledged teenagers on your hands, Deidre."

Mom didn't look amused. "Don't think we're not going to discuss y'all sneaking away from the River Walk," she told us grimly. "But that can wait. Why would someone take Lavender Adams? Did she know this young man?"

"No." Caitlyn glanced at me. "Um, we think it might have something to do with that key ring."

"What?" she and Aunt Cheryl said at the same time. Mom looked startled.

"I told them about it," Steve told his mother. "And

that's not all. I think that guy followed me from here when I went to meet the twins."

"The same one who took Lavender?" Now Mom looked puzzled. "That seems odd."

"Not really," I said. "Steve told us the man who delivered the key ring was worried he might be intercepted. Like someone wanted to grab it before it got to you."

Cait nodded. "So our kidnapper must be the interceptor, right?"

"Maybe." Aunt Cheryl looked thoughtful. "But why take your friend?"

"We think he was trying to find out where Mom is," I said. "Or something like that, anyway. Maybe he even thought he could trade Lav for information about the key ring."

"Sounds a little farfetched." Aunt Cheryl glanced at Mom. "But I suppose stranger things have happened, hmm?"

Mom sighed. "Good point. Girls, we need to find Lavender. Have you, er, seen anything that might help?"

"Yes!" Caitlyn answered immediately. "That's

why we went to El Mercado . . ."

As she described her vision, I shot a look toward Steve and Aunt Cheryl. It still felt a little strange to be talking about the Sight in front of them.

But when my sister finished, I was ready to take my turn. "I had a couple of visions about Lav, too," I said.

"Wait!" Cait said before I could continue. "I didn't tell them about the other one. I saw Lavender kissing Biff on the bus, remember?" She smiled. "Hey, that must mean we're going to find her, right? Otherwise she wouldn't be on the bus to be doing any kissing—I'm pretty sure that happens on the way home, since it's dark outside in the vision."

Mom was already shaking her head. "Things don't always work that way, though, do they?" she said. "You two saw me losing my job, too—and that never happened."

"Because we changed the future," I finished with a sigh.

Steve looked impressed. "Y'all can change the future?"

Caitlyn looked crestfallen. "Sometimes. But

usually it's to stop something bad from happening—like Mom losing her job, or Lavender's dog getting hit by a car, or Emily getting hurt doing something stupid . . ."

"But the point is, the future isn't set until it happens," Mom said. "No matter what you girls see, it can always play out differently." She shrugged. "At least that's how John explained it to me once," she added softly.

I traded a quick look with Caitlyn. Even now, Mom hardly ever mentioned our father's name.

"Whoa." Steve put his hands to his head in the universal symbol for having his mind blown. I knew how he felt.

"The point is, the kissing vision probably isn't related," I said. "But I had one that might be. I saw Lav and Cait in a shop or something."

"What happened in your vision?" Steve leaned forward, looking fascinated. Now that he was in on the secret, he barely seemed weirded out by it anymore.

I shrugged. "Lav looked annoyed. And then she

threw a fashion magazine at Cait." I glanced around at the others, who looked underwhelmed. "But that was it."

"Are you sure it has to do with the kidnapping?" Mom asked.

"I guess not." I bit my lip, trying to recall more about the vision. "Only wait—I'm pretty sure Lav was wearing the same outfit she is today. And she doesn't repeat her outfits too often, you know? What if it was showing me where she's being held prisoner?"

Caitlyn looked dubious. "I suppose it's possible," she said. "But why am I there, too?"

"It could be showing the moment you—I mean we—find her," Aunt Cheryl said. "Although I'm not sure why your friend would react by throwing a magazine."

"That's because you don't know Lavender."

Mom was pacing again. "This could be important. What else can you tell me about the location you saw, Cassie?"

"Not much." I closed my eyes, still trying to

remember more. "I think there were some weird posters on the wall, maybe?"

Mom stopped pacing and pulled out her phone. "Who are you calling?" Aunt Cheryl asked.

"Verity." Mom tapped the phone, and we could all hear ringing as the speaker phone came on. "The woman's annoying, but she might be able to—"

"Deidre?" Grandmother Lockwood's crisp British voice came over the speaker. "What is it?"

"Hello, Verity," Mom said. "We have a bit of a problem . . ."

She explained what had happened, with Cait and Steve and me adding a few words here and there. Granny Lockwood didn't say much until we'd all finished.

"Cassandra, you need to remember more details," she said firmly. "The best way to do that is with a focusing object. Do you have the talisman?"

I touched the necklace, which was tucked under my shirt. "I'm already wearing it."

"Hmm." She paused for a moment. "You said you're at your aunt's home? Is there anything there that might provide extra energy to help you relive your vision?"

I knew what she meant immediately. She'd been working with us to harness our powers. One of the exercises involved using multiple focusing objects to strengthen what we saw. For instance, she'd brought along a worn old wool scarf that had belonged to our father. We'd used several other family heirlooms, too. Granny L had explained that anything a Lockwood happened to be touching while having a vision would retain some of that energy. We'd been able to use that kind of energy to repeat a vision, or to make new visions stronger—and even to have visions about people we weren't even touching, like some of the ones about our father.

"I don't think so," I said. "I mean, Aunt Cheryl is Mom's sister. She wouldn't have anything here that belonged to our dad, if that's what you mean."

Aunt Cheryl gasped loudly. "Wait," she blurted out. "Actually, there is something like that here."

"What?" Granny Lockwood said sharply. "Who's speaking?"

"It's Cheryl—my sister," Mom replied. She gulped and reached into her pocket. "And she's right. I do have something of John's here . . ." She pulled out something small that glinted under the overhead light.

"Is that—" Caitlyn began.

"The key ring!" I jumped up and hurried over to see. "This was our dad's?"

Mom nodded and sighed. "I gave it to him on our first date," she said. "It was sort of a joke. I had no idea he'd kept it all these years. Not until Cheryl called the other day."

"But you're sure it's the same key ring, right?" Aunt Cheryl said.

"I'm sure." Mom clenched her hand into a fist, hiding the key ring from view again.

"Can we hold it?" Caitlyn asked hesitantly.

"Yes, hand it over, Deidre." I'd almost forgotten that our grandmother was still on speaker phone until her voice rang out again. "If the people who took John have the girls' friend, you need to find her before they do something desperate."

Mom nodded, handing me the key ring. I glanced at it, turning it over in my palm. One side showed the British flag, as Steve had mentioned. On the back, there were words scratched in the metal:

♥

U from UK to CA. JTL

"JTL," I said. "John Thompson Lockwood."

Caitlyn was peering over my shoulder. "Our dad inscribed this?"

Mom shrugged, confused. "That inscription is new," she said. "It wasn't there when I gave it to him."

"It looks like it was done recently." Steve was looking over my other shoulder by now. "See? The rest of the thing is kind of grimy, but that part's shiny."

Caitlyn and I stared at each other. "So maybe—" she began.

"What's going on?" Grandmother Lockwood's voice broke in again. "Did you give Cassandra the item, Deidre?"

"Yes." Mom sounded annoyed. "Now what?"

"Now she must focus. Cassandra, concentrate on whatever you recall of that vision."

"Okay." I closed my eyes, feeling self-conscious with everyone watching me. But I did my best to do as Granny L said. I thought about Lav, and the magazine. For a long moment nothing happened.

"What do you see?" Steve asked.

I shook my head and opened my eyes. "Nothing," I said, shifting the key ring to my other hand. "I just—"

I gasped, cutting myself off as a vision hit me like a ton of bricks. Aunt Cheryl's spare bedroom faded away, and instead I found myself looking at a much larger room—a kitchen. It was super fancy, with marble countertops and stuff.

The only person in the room was a man in a suit. For a second I couldn't figure out why he looked sort of familiar.

Then I remembered. He was the older man in a vision that Caitlyn and I had had during one of our training sessions with Granny Lockwood. Our father had been in that vision, too. This other guy had handed him something—maybe that key ring? I wasn't sure . . .

"Cass?" someone said. I think it was Aunt Cheryl. In any case, it broke me from the vision. I staggered over and collapsed on the edge of the bed, gulping air and feeling weird, as I always did after a vision.

"Did it work?" Caitlyn hurried over and sat down beside me. "Did you see Lav and me again?"

"N-no," I stammered. "I saw a totally different scene."

"What was it, Cassandra?" Granny L demanded. "Was John there?"

"No." I frowned. "It was the other guy—the one we saw with him in that other vision."

Cait caught on right away. "The older man in the nice suit?"

"The boring suit, yeah." I dropped the key ring on the bedspread, then wiped my sweaty palm on my leggings. "Only our dad wasn't there this time. The old guy was in some enormous kitchen, getting ready to take out the trash or something."

"Huh?" Aunt Cheryl blinked at me. "You had a vision of someone taking out the trash?"

"I guess." I shrugged. "First he loaded some flat tin cans into a garbage bag."

"Flat?" Caitlyn echoed. "You mean smushed, like some people do with soda cans?"

"No, flat shaped." I indicated the size of the cans with my hands. "Like the kind that fishy-type stuff comes in—anchovies or whatever. I guess they were stinky, too, because he made a 'yuck' face as he did it. After that, he swept some big, bright blue feathers into the bag, too."

"That's it?" Steve looked less than impressed.

"Interesting," Granny L said. "But we're wasting time. Cassandra, try again. This time, focus harder."

I frowned at the phone. "I was focusing," I said. "It just didn't work. It's not like you even know exactly how this stuff works—you admitted it yourself."

"Cassie," Mom said warningly.

Caitlyn grabbed the key ring from where I'd dropped it. "Here, I'll try to help," she said, reaching for my hand. "Maybe with both of us concentrating . . ."

I didn't hear the rest of what she said. Because the second she touched my hand, another vision practically bowled me over.

No, not another vision—the same one, the one with Lavender and Caitlyn. And this time I could see every detail of the shop clearly.

After a second Caitlyn fell back, losing her grip on me. "Whoa!" she exclaimed. "I think I just saw it—the vision."

"Yeah, me too." I stared at her. "It was the same as before, only way more vivid. You and Lav were in some shop—"

"Not a shop," Caitlyn corrected. "I think it was a hair salon. I saw blow-dryers and stuff in the background."

I nodded, realizing she was right. "Yeah. And there were weird posters on the wall, just like I thought."

"What kind of posters?" Mom asked. "Tell us exactly what you saw, girls. Maybe if we give a description of the place to the local police, they'll know where it is."

"There were four or five of them," Cait said. "They showed ladies with big, fancy hairdos."

"Uh-huh," I said. "Only their hair was dyed these wild colors—a different shade in each poster. Like, one was bright magenta, another was lime green—"

Aunt Cheryl sat bolt upright. "Hang on—I've seen those posters. I know that place!"

"You do?" Mom demanded.

Aunt Cheryl nodded. "It's a hair salon up near the Farmer's Market," she said. "A fairly tacky one, honestly. I went there once because I had a coupon." She touched her hair, which she wore in a chin-length bob. "They almost ruined my mane."

Mom was already heading for the door. "Let's go."

9
CAITLYN

LIAM JUMPED TO his feet when we raced into the front room. "Did you bring the cookies?" he asked eagerly.

"Yeah." Buzz tossed a cookie into his mouth. "We already ate the ones you brought before, and Liam didn't get any."

"Sorry, dude." Brayden gave Liam a friendly punch on the shoulder.

Somehow I'd nearly forgotten that our friends were out there. Yikes! How were we supposed to explain what we were doing?

Mom obviously decided there was no need to

explain at all. She just headed straight for the door. "Stay here, kids," she tossed over her shoulder as she grabbed her jacket. "Ms. Church should arrive soon. My sister will wait with you."

"Huh?" Megan jumped up, too. "Wait, where are you going?"

"Hold on, Deidre," Aunt Cheryl put in. "I'm coming with you."

"No, you're not," Mom said.

"Yes, I am." Aunt Cheryl might be the only person in the world who isn't afraid to stand up to Mom when she's acting all strict and scarymama. "How else are you going to get there? I'll drive us." She glanced around the room. "All of us."

Suddenly everyone seemed to realize that something was happening. The entire group gathered up phones and jackets and rushed for the door.

"Good thing Mom has the van," Steve commented.

I'd almost forgotten about the van. We'd all made fun of it for years. The thing was huge. Still, there was no way all fifteen of us could fit.

Aunt Cheryl grabbed two sets of keys from the

little table near the door. She tossed one set to Mom.

"You can take Charles's car," she said. "Follow me."

It was a tight squeeze, but we did it. Cassie, Megan, and Biff rode with Mom in Uncle Charles's hatchback, with Brayden and his cast in the back. The rest of us went in the van.

The salon was only a few blocks from El Mercado, but it might as well have been on a different planet. Instead of the tidy, tourist-packed streets, there were just a few warehouses and run-down businesses. A homeless man was slumped on the sidewalk, snoring loudly.

"Ew, what are we doing here?" Abby exclaimed.

Liam peered out the window. "Are we getting our hair cut?" he joked.

I looked over his shoulder. One of the businesses on the block was a beauty salon. The sign was small and dingy, but there were several people inside.

"We think Lavender might be here," I told Liam and Bianca quietly.

Emily overheard me and gasped. "Really?" she cried. "Let's go get her!"

"Stop!" Aunt Cheryl exclaimed.

But it was too late. Everyone was pouring out of the van. I shrugged and followed.

Mom was climbing out of the car nearby. "Hold up, people!" she yelled. "Stay right here—the police are on their way."

"Oh, yeah? Can't handle it yourself, huh?" Gabe muttered with a sneer.

I wasn't sure whether Mom had heard him. If so, she wasn't letting on. Cassie and I had learned that most of the time the best way to handle Gabe was to ignore him.

Everyone started milling around near the van. I guessed we were making quite a ruckus. For one thing, the homeless guy woke up and stretched, peering at us curiously through a pair of dirty sunglasses.

Also, a woman came out of the beauty shop. She was a little older than Mom, with dark hair and a pinched, suspicious look on her face.

"Who are you?" she snapped. "This is a place of business, not a schoolyard. You're disturbing my customers with all this noise."

Mom stepped toward her, going into police officer mode, even though she wasn't wearing her uniform. "You work at this place?" she asked.

"I own this place." The woman crossed her arms over her chest. "Why?"

Mom put out her hand, and Megan handed over her phone. Mom held it up in front of the woman. "Have you seen this girl?"

Cassie sidled over to me. "Megs had a photo of Lav on her phone," she whispered.

I'd already figured that out. Now I was waiting to hear what the salon owner said.

"No," the woman said, barely glancing toward the phone. "Now if you'll excuse me, I have customers waiting."

"Hold on." Mom's scarymama voice could stop a runaway train. The woman paused. "This girl is missing, and a witness placed her at your salon."

"A witness?" Abby whispered loudly to Emily. "What witness?"

I winced. Mom was so intent on finding Lavender that she clearly didn't realize she was on the verge of giving away our secret!

"Nobody," I whispered to Emily and Abby. "It's, um, a police technique."

The salon owner was glaring at Mom, looking mulish. Meanwhile the homeless guy had lumbered to his feet.

"Hey," he called in a raspy voice. "You kids looking for the other rich girl?"

Megan spun to face him. "What did you say?"

"Kids, get back in the car," Mom ordered.

But Cassie took a step toward the homeless man. "Did you see a girl our age?" she asked. "White girl, dark hair, blue shirt?"

"Sure." The man's smile was toothless and rather cagey. "I'll show you where she is for a dollar."

"Get out of here," the salon owner snapped. "Ignore him," she told Mom. "He hangs around all the time trying to trick people into giving him money."

"Hmm." Mom glanced at the homeless guy. "Sir," she addressed him brusquely, "if you've really seen a girl around here, you'd better tell me about it. The police will be here shortly, and they'll be very interested as well."

The guy held up both hands in a gesture of surrender. "No, never mind," he said. "The lady's right, I don't know nothing."

"Wait." Cassie shot an annoyed look at Mom. "You're scaring him off, and he might be our only witness!" She stuck her hand in her pocket and pulled out a dollar bill. "Here—now show us, okay?"

The man grabbed the dollar eagerly, shoving it deep into the pocket of his dirty gray pants. "This way," he said, shambling toward the corner of the building.

"Stop!" the salon lady exclaimed as we all followed. "This is private property. I'll call the police!"

"No need," Mom told her. "As I mentioned, they're already on the way."

Aunt Cheryl was still trying to convince our friends to stay back. But I was right behind Cassie and Mom, who were right behind the homeless man.

"I'm serious!" The salon lady continued to bluster the whole way down the alley. Soon we reached a window at the back of the building.

"She's in there," the homeless guy said.

I rushed forward, pressing my face to the window. Cassie was doing the same.

"It's her!" she shouted. "Hey, Lav! Out here!"

We were looking into what appeared to be a small apartment behind the shop. Lavender was inside, lounging on a dingy plaid sofa reading a magazine. She looked up when Cass knocked on the window.

Before I could see her reaction, I heard sudden movement behind me. It was the salon owner—she was taking off back toward the street.

"Hey!" I yelled. "She's running away!"

Mom pushed past me at a run. "Stop right there!" she shouted.

The woman had a pretty good head start. But I guessed Mom's cop voice really carries. Because a second later, the B Boys appeared at the end of the alley. When they saw the woman running toward them, they linked arms, forming a human chain to block her way.

"Move!" she shrieked, skidding to a stop to keep

herself from plowing into them. "What are you doing?"

That was all it took for Mom to catch up. She grabbed the woman by the arm and bustled her around the corner and into the beauty shop. Aunt Cheryl made the others stay outside, but she let Cassie and me past.

Two women were in the stylists' chairs when we entered, while a third was leaning against the counter nearby. All three of them stared as Mom marched the owner past them.

I glanced around the salon. "Look, there are the posters," I whispered to my sister.

"Yeah." She wrinkled her nose. "They're even weirder in real life."

There was a door at the back of the salon. Mom insisted that the owner unlock it and let her through. Beyond was a dimly lit hallway, with several doors opening off it.

"Stay here, girls," Mom ordered sternly. "Just in case."

Just in case of what? I wasn't sure, but she was

using that scarymama voice again, so I obeyed. Cassie did too, though she leaned so far forward through the doorway that I was afraid she'd tip over.

"What's going on?" One of the customers came toward us, hanging on to her protective cape to stop it from slipping off. "Who is that with Anna?"

"Our mother," I told her.

I kept watching as the salon owner unlocked another door at the far end of the hallway. A second later Lavender burst out, waving a magazine and yelling something about her phone.

"Oh, right," Cassie said. "I almost forgot the one about her phone getting smashed. No wonder she didn't answer any texts."

I'd mostly forgotten about that vision, too. But there was no time to ponder it. Lavender was barreling toward us, still yelling. I took a few quick steps back so she wouldn't run me over.

"I can't believe this!" she was shouting. "Did you find the lying creep who locked me in here? Because he said he was taking me to a sample sale, but instead he dragged me to this gross place and broke my phone . . ."

As she continued to rant, I leaned toward Cassie. "What's a sample sale?" I whispered.

"It's when designers sell off extra clothes super cheap." She sounded distracted. "I've never been to one, but they're supposed to be awesome."

I supposed that explained why I'd had a vision of Lavender getting kidnapped, even though I usually only saw good stuff happening. In the vision, Lavender must still have thought the guy was dragging her off to that imaginary sample sale. Which would have been a good thing in her eyes.

". . . and so I was stuck in there for, like, hours," Lavender was complaining. "With nothing to eat, and nothing to do."

"Except read magazines, right?" I joked, trying to lighten the mood a little.

It didn't work. Lavender spun around and glared at me. "Are you kidding, Caitlyn?" she snapped. "All the stupid magazines back there are like three months out of date. Ew!"

With that, she hurled the magazine she was clutching at my head. I sidestepped, and it fell to the floor.

Lavender glared at Cassie, too. "It took you guys long enough to find me!" Then she blinked at the homeless man, who had followed us into the salon. "Ew, who's that?"

I frowned. "As a matter of fact, he's the person who helped us find you," I replied, a little annoyed by the way she was making faces at the homeless guy. Okay, yeah, he smelled a little, and his ragged clothes weren't exactly the type of high fashion that Lavender Adams preferred. Still, she didn't have to be so rude all the time, right?

"Yeah," Cassie told her. "He saw you through the window and brought us to rescue you."

"Really?" Lavender blinked, suddenly looking much less annoyed. "Oh. Um, thanks." She stuck her hand in her pocket and pulled out a wad of cash. She took a step closer to the homeless man, wrinkled her nose in distaste, flung the money at him, and then rushed past.

"Whoa!" The man's eyes widened as he bent to pick up the money, which was fluttering to the floor. "Tell your friend thanks!"

Just then there was a commotion of engines and the whoop of a siren outside. The cops had arrived.

"Come with me," Mom told the salon owner. "I'm sure the officers will have a few questions for you—especially about whether you know the young man they already have in custody."

Suddenly the woman looked nervous. "What? No, please. It was all me," she babbled. "My son didn't have anything to do with this!"

"Her son?" Cass echoed as Mom dragged the woman out. "I guess that's why she let him hide Lav here."

"Yeah." I smiled at her. "And we didn't even have to change the future this time to save the day."

AN HOUR OR two later, Cassie, Mom, and I were finally back at Aunt Cheryl's house. We'd spent most of the time in between at the precinct waiting around while the paperwork got done. Another couple of cars had gone to return Lavender and the others to the main group up at the River Walk, but we'd asked to come here.

Cassie checked the time on her phone as we knocked on the door. "We can't stay here long—the buses are leaving in an hour."

"I know." Mom nodded to Steve, who'd just opened the door. "But first we need to talk this over."

Soon we were inside. Uncle Charles was there by now, too, looking big and comfortable and friendly as he always did, though he wasn't quite as smiley as usual. "Everything okay?" he asked when we entered, his concerned brown eyes sweeping over all three of us.

"Fine." Mom shot a look toward Aunt Cheryl. "Did you . . . ?" she began.

"I filled him in," Aunt Cheryl said. "But never mind, y'all will need to leave soon. Want something to eat?"

"No thanks," Mom said before Cassie or I could respond. I was a little disappointed. Lunch seemed, like, a million years ago, and my stomach grumbled at the thought of Aunt Cheryl's corn bread with Uncle Charles's homemade blackberry jam.

I forgot about eating as Mom started telling the others what had gone down at the precinct. ". . . and the man they brought in still isn't talking about why he lured Lavender away from her friends, even after she ID'd him," she was saying. "So officially, we still don't know why he did it."

"Except that we totally do," Cassie said. "I'm sure he came to try to get that key chain back."

"But why?" I wondered aloud. "What's so important about it?" I glanced at Mom. "Except to you and our dad, I mean."

"Good question." Mom stared into space. "I can't imagine how anyone else would even know about it. I'd nearly forgotten it myself."

Steve perched on the arm of the sofa. "So did you figure out what that message means?" he asked Mom. "Heart you from UK to CA—what's up with that?"

"Well, John and I met in England—the UK." Mom glanced at Cass and me. "And we were living in

California when the girls were born. That must be what it means." She frowned at Steve, as if not quite satisfied with her own theory. "Or if it's not, then I have no idea why John—or someone else—would scratch those words on there . . ."

She looked so perturbed that I stepped over and patted her on the arm. Just as I did, the room disappeared just long enough for a brief vision to take its place—a vision of Mom smiling and stroking a big, colorful parrot.

Weird. But probably not worth mentioning, I figured, since Vision Mom had looked kind of hot and sweaty and was dressed in shorts and a thin T-shirt, which meant it probably wasn't going to come true anytime soon.

See? I'm learning from Cassie, I thought with a slight smile, making a mental note to tell my sister about the new vision later. *She's always telling me that fashion is super important—and I guess occasionally, it actually is!*

10
CASSIE

"... AND IT WAS, like, super horrible and gross, of course," Lavender said. "But I wasn't scared at all."

I sighed. She was leaning forward against the back of my seat, which meant she was pretty much shouting directly in my ear. She'd been regaling the entire bus with the tale of her adventures since the city limits.

If she keeps it up, it's going to be a looooong ride back to Aura, I thought with a muffled sigh.

Still, I couldn't really blame her for wanting to talk about it. Especially since nobody—including

Lav—seemed quite sure what had happened or why. Most kids were obviously assuming it was some kind of random big-city crime.

Whatever. I was just glad nobody had figured out that Caitlyn and I were connected to the incident. And I was pretty convinced that we were. We'd spent a little while at Aunt Cheryl's going over everything we knew, but we'd had to skedaddle before we came up with any new theories. At least any that made much sense.

I was sitting by the window for the trip home, with Cait on the aisle where she could talk to her nerdy friends, who had ended up across the way. Brayden and his crutches were two seats behind them, which meant there wasn't much chance I'd get to talk to him anyway. So much for my big romantic day with my trip buddy . . .

But I tried not to think about that. Instead, I tuned out Lavender's voice and stared out the window. It was dark outside, the flashing headlights of passing cars making it hard to see much of the landscape. Resting my head against the squishy pleather seat, I gazed up toward the sky instead. It was a clear night, with lots of stars, though the moon wasn't up yet.

I yawned, wondering how long it would take us to get home. Then I blinked. Whoa. Had I really just thought of Aura as "home"? I wasn't quite sure how to feel about that. But maybe . . . maybe it was okay?

As I was pondering what that meant, I realized that Lav's chatter had finally stopped. Good. I yawned again, closing my eyes and trying to let myself drift off to sleep. But my brain was spinning along even faster than the tires on the bus, still trying to make sense of everything that had happened today.

Suddenly my eyes flew open again as someone behind me kicked the back of my seat. A second later came a muffled giggle. Huh? I rolled my eyes, wondering if Lavender had talked Megan into trying to play pranks on me or something.

"Very funny, guys," I muttered, craning my neck to get a look over the high seat back.

I was just in time to see that Megan had disappeared, replaced by Biff—who was just leaning over to give Lav a short, sweet kiss on the lips!

Vision, I thought, quickly dropping back into my seat so they wouldn't catch me peeking. The Sight had struck again—Cait had seen that kiss happen days ago.

That was the thing about the visions. We never knew which ones were important and which were just part of normal life, like that kiss. Not even with my sister getting all the good stuff and me getting the bad stuff. Sometimes it was hard to tell the two apart, or to guess exactly what the visions were trying to show us. Which made it hard to try to stop the bad stuff from happening.

But we had to try. I realized that now. Because the more we tried, the better we got at this. I mean, if we'd wanted to, I was pretty sure that my sister and I could have stopped that kiss vision from coming true. All I would have had to do was switch seats with Megan. Or maybe Caitlyn could have distracted Biff somehow.

We hadn't done any of that, though. Because that kiss didn't really matter. But some of our visions did— like the other ones about Lav, which had helped us find her and stop something way worse from happening.

And the ones about our dad, too. The trouble was, those visions were all a lot more complicated and hard to figure out than a simple kiss . . .

Still, we have to try, I reminded myself. Sitting there staring out into the vast Texas night, it suddenly felt like a big responsibility, one I wasn't sure I was ready for . . .

I felt Cait shuffle beside me and turned to find her gazing at me with a thoughtful expression on her face. Was she having the same kinds of thoughts as I was? Maybe it was that twintuition thing kicking in again.

Cait opened her mouth as if she wanted to say something. But just then Brayden appeared in the aisle behind her.

"Hey," he said, leaning on the back of the seat since he wasn't using his crutches. "Caitlyn, do you mind if we trade seats for a bit?" He shot her a slightly bashful grin. "Uh, I think my crutches are lonely."

Cait giggled. "Sure, no problem. I'll go keep them company." She waggled her eyebrows dramatically at me, which I really hoped Brayden didn't see. Then she slid out of the seat.

Brayden took her place. "Hey, Cassie," he said.

"Hey." I glanced at the bandages on his arms. "You sore from that spill you took earlier?"

"Nah." He shrugged. "It was no biggie." He cleared his throat and looked past me out the bus window. "Long day, though, huh?"

"Kind of."

He nodded. "Anyway, uh, I just wanted to say thanks. You know, for helping me get around and stuff." He waved a hand toward his cast. "That was cool of you."

"Oh. Sure, no problem." I hadn't really done all that much except carry his crutches that one time. But if he thought I was Miss Helpful, I wasn't going to argue. "It was fun."

"Yeah." He shifted in his seat. "Anyway, I'm glad we were, you know, partners or whatever."

"Me, too." I was still a little distracted by my earlier thoughts. But not too distracted to notice that he seemed nervous. Which really wasn't like him. Could *I* be making him nervous?

"Anyway," he blurted out, "uh, Biff was talking about getting a group together to see that new horror movie tomorrow night. It's playing in Six Oaks."

"Yeah? Sounds cool."

He smiled. "So you're in? Cool."

Had he just asked me out? I wasn't sure. But going to the movies with my friends sounded like just the break I needed from all this Sight stuff. Especially after everything that had happened today . . . I shivered slightly at the memory of how it had all played out. The key chain with those words scratched on it—what could it mean? The nasty guy who'd grabbed Lav—what was he after, and why? And most of all, my father. Could he really be alive? What else could those visions be trying to tell us?

I almost forgot that Brayden was still there until he scooted a little closer and elbowed me gently. "Hey, you okay?" he asked in a soft voice. "What are you thinking about?"

I glanced over at him, forcing a smile. If only I could tell him the truth. It was hard lying to my friends all the time—but I didn't have much choice, did I?

"Nothing, just looking forward to the movie," I said, doing my best to sound normal.

"Yeah, me too." He leaned a little closer. His eyes were locked on mine, and suddenly the air around us felt strange, as if little electric currents were pulling us together.

I held my breath. Was he about to kiss me, like Biff and Lav? Too bad I hadn't had a vision to give me a hint about that . . .

"Hey!" Lavender's loud voice suddenly burst out just above our heads. "Bray, did you ask her about the movie?"

Suddenly the spell was shattered. Brayden leaned back. I looked up to see Lav grinning down at us.

"Yeah, I'm in," I told her.

She chattered at us about the movie for a few seconds, then ducked away out of sight. I shot Brayden a sidelong look, wondering what he was thinking. Again, too bad my visions couldn't tell me useful things like that once in a while!

He was just sitting there, drumming his hands on his legs, not really looking at me. I sighed and leaned back, mentally cursing Lav and her terrible timing.

Then Brayden cleared his throat. "So listen, Cassie," he said. "Um, about that movie . . ."

"Yeah?" I prompted when he paused for, like, a really long time.

"I was wondering, I mean, I was hoping, that is . . ." He cleared his throat again. "So, how about if we sit together? You and me, I mean."

I smiled. "Sure. That sounds great." I almost added *it's a date* but stopped myself just in time.

"Cool." He sounded relieved. Then a moment later, he reached over and took my hand.

For a second I wasn't sure what he was doing. But when he squeezed, I squeezed back. We sat there for a while, not saying anything, just looking out the window at the passing night with our hands intertwined.

Okay, it wasn't a kiss. But it was really nice. And the best part? No visions at all. Whew!

Because truth be told? I was ready for a serious break from all that. Although I was pretty sure I wasn't going to get one anytime soon.

11
CAITLYN

"RISE AND SHINE, baby doll," Cassie sang out, yanking back the curtain over our bedroom window.

"Urgh!" I mumbled as the bright morning sun poured in, practically blinding me as I peeled one eye open. "What time is it?"

"Not sure."

I was too tired to actually roll my eyes, but I wanted to. Cassie was probably lying about not knowing the time. Since it was an in-service day, I'd planned to sleep in. Not leap out of bed at the crack of dawn like my sister always did.

"Seriously, get up," she said. "Granny Lockwood's here."

That woke me up the rest of the way. I sat up, tossing my covers aside. "She's here now?"

"Uh-huh. She wants to talk to us about what happened yesterday."

I got dressed in record time. Soon Cass and I were sitting at the kitchen table with our grandmother and Mom. Grandmother Lockwood looked grim, although to be honest, she always looks a little bit that way.

"Tell me everything that happened yesterday," she ordered, staring from me to Cass and back again.

"Okay." Cassie poured herself a glass of OJ. "First I brushed my teeth—"

"This is no time for fooling around, Cassandra," Grandmother Lockwood interrupted sharply.

"For once, I agree with your grandmother," Mom put in. "We need to take this seriously, girls."

That was kind of a change of pace for Mom. Up until now, she hadn't wanted much to do with this whole Sight thing. Then again, I couldn't blame her. Her long-lost husband might be alive—that was a big deal, for real!

"Well, you already heard about the visions that Cassie and I had about Lavender, right?" I began.

"Yes. But tell me again." Grandmother Lockwood leaned forward. "Don't leave out any details."

Grandmother Lockwood asked a bunch of questions, especially when we got to the part about the key chain.

Finally she seemed satisfied. "All right," she said. "Now let's return to your training."

"Hold on." Mom sounded wary. "Verity, we talked about this so-called training of yours . . ."

"Deidre, we don't have time to go through all this again, all right? The girls could be our only way to find John before it's—" She cut herself off, shooting us a wary look.

"Before it's too late?" Cassie guessed. "That's what you were going to say, isn't it? What do you know that you're not telling us? Because none of this is making much sense."

"No kidding," I murmured.

"You might as well tell them," Mom told Grandmother Lockwood. "They're in this now—they should know everything."

"Who is that lady, and what did she do with our mother?" Cassie murmured.

"Fine," Grandmother Lockwood said with an impatient sigh. "Girls, my people are still working on finding out more about John's disappearance—and that key chain."

"And?" Cass prompted.

"And they're working on a few leads that seem to indicate that he could be in danger," the old woman said grimly. "Now that word has leaked out that he might be alive, it seems someone doesn't really want him to be found."

"Like that guy who kidnapped Lavender?" I guessed. "He knew about the key chain." I shot Cassie a look. "At least we think he did."

We'd already told Mom and Grandmother Lockwood about that, and they both nodded. "Yes, I'm sure it's all connected," Grandmother Lockwood said. "My people are trying to figure out who that man might be."

Just then the phone rang. "Don't say or do anything important until I get back," Mom ordered. Then she hurried out to the living room to answer.

Grandmother Lockwood hardly seemed to notice. She pulled Dad's worn wool scarf out of her purse. "Let's get started. Where's the talisman?"

"Here," Cassie said, pulling the key-shaped pendant out from under her collar.

"But Mom wants us to wait for her," I said at the same time.

"Time is of the essence, Caitlyn," Grandmother Lockwood snapped. "Please do as I say."

I might not be a rebel like Cassie can be. But I have my stubborn moments sometimes.

"Okay." I crossed my arms and leaned back in my chair. "But it's not so urgent that we can't give Mom two seconds to get off the phone."

Have you ever heard that saying about someone's eyes shooting flames? Well, I always thought that was kind of a goofy saying. But right now, as Grandmother Lockwood glared at me? I kind of got it.

Luckily Mom hurried back in right at that moment. "That was the San Antonio police," she announced. "The perp finally confessed."

"He did?" Cassie sat up straight. "He admitted to kidnapping Lav?"

"More or less." Mom took her seat. "Although he claims he was going to let her go either way. It seems he's a San Antonio local, well known to the department thanks to a pretty long rap sheet—mostly petty stuff like shoplifting, some breaking and entering, drug offenses, that sort of thing. So he was willing to cut a deal once he realized he wasn't getting off scot-free."

"What did he say?" Grandmother Lockwood demanded. "Who was he working for?"

Mom sighed. "That's the trouble—he didn't seem to know. He gave a name, but it turned out to be fake. So all we know is that some unknown person hired him to get that key chain back before it got to me." She shrugged. "Obviously, he failed."

"So he was just a hired thug," I said.

"Yes." Mom shrugged again. "The Lavender thing was his idea, apparently—he was still hoping to get a paycheck out of the whole disaster somehow. But then he got cold feet. He claimed he was about to call his mother to let Lavender go when y'all accosted him at El Mercado."

"Never mind." Grandmother Lockwood picked up the scarf again. "Back to work . . ."

This time Mom didn't protest. Grandmother Lockwood had me and Cassie touch various objects and focus on Dad to try to bring on visions about him. Her techniques had worked in San Antonio the day before, and a few other times in the past, but today we weren't having much luck. After half an hour or so, we were all feeling a little frustrated.

"I thought you knew what you were doing, Verity," Mom said. "This seems like a waste of time. According to John, the visions come whenever they come, and there's not much you can do to change that."

Cassie and I traded a surprised look. How much had our father told her about the Sight? At first we'd assumed the answer to that was a big fat nothing. But maybe not so much . . .

"You're not helping, Deidre," Grandmother Lockwood snapped back. "Girls, try again."

"ARE YOU GOING to get popcorn?" Liam asked. "We could split one if you guys like extra butter."

"Sure, I'm in," I said. Liam, Bianca, and I had just walked into the movie theater at the Six Oaks Galleria. Cassie and her friends were there, too. They'd decided to get a group together to see the latest blockbuster, and when the B Boys had invited Liam, he'd invited Bianca and me.

I wasn't sure how Cassie felt about us crashing her evening with the popular crowd. She hadn't said much to me since around lunchtime, when Grandmother Lockwood had finally released us from training. Then Lavender had called with some new bit of juicy gossip about Sakiko Star, and a few minutes later Cass had gone rushing off to Megan's house.

Not that there was much to talk about, since Grandmother Lockwood's training exercises hadn't worked this time. Cassie and I hadn't had a single

vision all day. It figured—when we didn't want to
see stuff, we did. And now that we hoped to find out
more about our dad? Zippo.

I got in line at the snack bar with my friends. Lavender and Biff were right in front of us.

"Yo, dude." Biff held out his hand to Liam for a
fist bump. "This movie's going to be epic!"

"I hope it's not too scary," Lavender said with a
dramatic shiver.

"Don't worry. I'll protect you from all the mon-
sters." Biff slung his arm around her shoulders, and
she giggled. Okay, I wasn't the world's biggest Lavender Adams fan, and I didn't know Biff very well
at all. But I had to admit, it was sort of cute how
couple-y they were acting tonight.

And they weren't the only ones. My gaze wandered a little farther up the line to where my sister
was standing with Brayden. They weren't quite as
obvious as the other pair, but I could tell they were
getting closer. Majorly adorable!

*I bet Mom and Dad were adorable back in the day,
too*, I thought, flashing again to the key chain. How

cute was it that he'd kept something like that all these years? I only wished we knew what the message on it meant . . .

Just then Emily hurried past me toward the front of the line. "Hey, let me cut, okay?" she said to Brayden, poking him in the arm.

"No cuts," Cassie spoke up with a smirk. "Sorry not sorry."

"Come on," Emily wheedled, ignoring my sister and smiling up at Brayden.

"You heard her." Brayden shrugged and grinned. "Sorry not sorry."

Emily frowned. "Thanks for nothing, Brayden," she snapped, giving him a little shrug. Then she spun on her heel and stormed off.

Meanwhile Cassie turned, scanning the line until she spotted me. She waggled her eyebrows, then nodded toward Emily.

Huh? It took me a second to catch on. Then I got it. She'd had a vision about Emily a while ago. I guessed her expression meant it had just come true.

But who cared about some dumb random vision? We needed to see something more important than Emily flirting with Brayden—before it was too late, as Grandmother Lockwood had said.

The movie turned out to be pretty boring, so I spent most of it going over all the clues in my head, trying to figure out something we'd missed. Trying to figure out what the visions were trying to tell us about our dad.

But no luck. By the ending credits, I remained just as perplexed as ever.

On the way out of the theater, Cassie caught up to me. "Did you see that?" she murmured. "With Ems earlier? That was my vision."

"Yeah, I got that," I said, still distracted by my own thoughts.

Cassie turned away. As she did, her elbow grazed my arm, and suddenly the real world faded out, replaced by a buzzing sound and the vision of Cassie standing on the beach, staring at the ocean, dressed in a cute bathing suit I'd never seen before.

I shook it off as soon as she moved away. Talk

about random! It was late fall—not exactly beach season. Obviously, whatever I'd just seen happened far in the future.

In other words, random. And no help at all.

12

CASSIE

OKAY, EVERYONE KNOWS I'm a morning person. But even I wasn't ready to crawl out of bed when Grandmother Lockwood arrived bright and early on Saturday morning. We'd been out late Friday night—after the movie, someone had suggested hitting up the food court at the mall for some late-night tacos. Miraculously, even Mom had okayed the plan, even though she was normally a freak about curfew. I wondered if Mom was cutting us some slack because of all the Sight stuff. She had to know it wasn't easy for us to deal with all that. She'd barely even yelled at us about the whole sneaking-away-from-River-Walk deal.

"For real?" Caitlyn mumbled as she staggered to her feet and squinted toward the window. "Is it even technically morning yet?"

"It's probably already, like, lunchtime in England," I said with a yawn. "Or maybe it's the middle of the night. I can never remember whether they're ahead of us or behind."

If Cait even heard me, she didn't show it. She was zombie-walking over to the dresser. "Come on," she said. "We should get out there. This is important."

"Yeah." Normally I make fun of her when she goes all serious like that. But this time I had to agree. Ever since our little talk the day before, I couldn't stop thinking about what Granny L had said: my sister and I might be the only chance to find our dad before it was too late. The pressure was too much.

Caitlyn and I got dressed and ready in record time, but even so, Granny L looked impatient when we hurried into the main room.

"Sit down, girls," she said. "Your mother will get you something to eat while we get started."

Mom had been sitting there drinking her coffee, and she shot Granny L an annoyed look. But she got up without a word and walked into the kitchen.

Which just went to show how serious things were. Mom always tells us she's not a short-order cook or a maid; Cait and I are supposed to deal with breakfast ourselves unless it's a special occasion. Which I supposed maybe this was . . .

Meanwhile, Granny L was digging around in a shopping bag on the floor beside her. "I've had my people in England ship over a few more things that might help," she told us. "Family heirlooms that could act as talismans."

I nodded along with Caitlyn. We already knew how that worked—sort of, anyway. Any object that had been in the possession of a Lockwood during a vision could be a talisman.

"Whoa, is that an actual *tiara*?" I blurted out as our grandmother set a glittery little filigreed crown on the table. "Those look like diamonds!"

"It belonged to your great-great-aunt Penelope Lockwood," she said. "I don't know if your father ever touched it, but never mind."

Next she pulled out a stack of wrinkled papers. "What's that?" Caitlyn asked.

"It's the correspondence I mentioned before," our grandmother replied. "The letters my investigators found—letters to your father from someone with the initials QJ. Some of them were destroyed, it seems, but what's left might be helpful somehow."

Mom heard Granny L and hurried out of the kitchen, spatula in hand. "Let me see," she said.

We all pored over the letters. They were hard to read—handwritten in spidery pen scribbles. But most of them seemed to involve this QJ guy begging our dad to come work for him.

"So who's QJ?" I wondered aloud, flipping over one of the pages to study the scrawled initials at the bottom of the note.

Granny L shrugged. "We're still trying to work that out," she said. "Now let's focus, please, girls."

I glanced at the pile of stuff she'd been unloading

onto the table while we were looking at the letters. Some of it was boring junk—a pair of gloves, some books, and random trinkets. But there was a jewel-encrusted gold cup there, too, and an emerald ring sitting next to the tiara I'd noticed earlier. Whoa. Exactly how rich were these British relatives of ours, anyway?

Caitlyn was still focused on the letters. "QJ," she said. "That's kind of an unusual initial—the Q part, I mean. Maybe we can figure out—"

"Leave the detective work to the professionals," Granny L snapped. "We have other work to do."

Caitlyn looked slightly wounded, but she dropped the note. "Okay, what do you want us to do?"

It turned out that she just wanted us to keep trying to have visions about our dad. We tried for a while, taking turns wearing the talisman and touching the other stuff. I even got to wear the tiara, which was cool. But at first none of it seemed to be working.

Then it did. Granny L had us loop the scarf around both our shoulders. I had the necklace on, and Cait was holding some of the other talismans.

This time, as soon as I touched her hand, a vision hit me hard and fast.

The kitchen faded away, along with Cait and Granny L and Mom and everything. Instead I found myself outdoors on a bright, sunny day. Sunlight sparkled over the ocean—I had a great view of it from atop a high, rocky cliff. I could see a ship in the distance, a pretty church off to the side with colorfully dressed people pouring out of it, horseback riders on the beach far below, gulls wheeling in the sky. It was beautiful!

Well, not all of it . . . Standing at the edge of the cliff were two men. One was my father, who was standing with his back to the cliff, facing me. The other guy had his back to me. I didn't pay much attention to him—I was totally focused on my dad. He looked terrified. His hands were up in front of him and he appeared to be talking rapidly, though as usual all I could hear was that annoying buzzing.

Then, suddenly, the other man lunged forward—and shoved at my father with the end of a cane! I screamed as he went tumbling backward, arms flailing helplessly as he fell over the edge of the cliff . . .

"Cassie! It's okay! Cass, snap out of it!" Caitlyn was shaking me as I returned to reality.

"Whoa," I said weakly. "That was intense . . ."

I told them what I'd seen. Granny L looked alarmed. "Who was the other man?" she demanded. "What did he look like?"

I shrugged. "I'm not sure. Sort of short, maybe? Dark hair I think—I don't know, I didn't get a very good look at him."

She didn't seem satisfied by that. "Let's try again," she said. "Perhaps if you focus, both of you will see it."

"So you didn't see anything?" I shot Cait a look. "Figures. You only see good stuff, right?" I shuddered. "Trust me, there was nothing good about what I just saw."

Well, except the part about seeing my dad again. But I didn't say it out loud.

"We need more information," Granny L insisted. "Girls, join hands."

But I pulled my hands away before my sister could grab them. "Hold on," I said. "Who says I even want to see that again?"

Grandmother Lockwood frowned at me. "Grow up, Cassandra. Don't you want to help your father? We have to try anything we can to find him!"

She had a point. I sighed and held out my hands. "Okay," I said to Caitlyn. "But don't say I didn't warn you . . ."

We must have tried to get that vision back for a good half hour, but nothing came. No visions at all. Nada.

"This is stupid," I said, shoving away the scarf and tiara. "It's not working."

"Maybe that's because you're not trying hard enough." My grandmother glared at me. "You have to focus, Cassandra. I know it's not pleasant, but—"

"How would you know that?" I retorted. "You're not the one who just watched your dad get, like, murdered or whatever."

"Cassie . . . ," Cait said softly.

"No, seriously!" I was over this—and definitely

over Granny L's attitude. "I never asked for this stupid Sight, okay? So don't tell me I'm not trying hard enough."

Mom had been sitting quietly through most of this, working on her third cup of coffee. Now she pushed her mug away and stood up.

"Maybe I can help," she said.

"You?" Granny L stared at her. "How?"

Mom shrugged. "I was married to John for years—surely that makes me at least as useful a talisman as some ratty old scarf, right?"

"That's not how it works," Granny L protested. "The idea is that energy is stored in these talismans. Objects he and other Lockwoods were touching during the visions. Just being around him isn't enough—that's why I didn't drag along the chandelier from the dining room or John's old childhood bicycle."

"Look, you said it yourself—we have to keep trying." Mom came around the table to stand between me and Cait. "Why not give it a whirl? What do we have to lose?"

Granny L still looked dubious. But she shrugged. "Fine. But keep touching the other items too, girls."

The three of us joined hands, with Mom in the middle. She squeezed so hard it almost hurt.

"Let's do this," she said. "Ready, girls?"

I barely heard her, because I was falling into another vision. Once again it was outside on a bright and sunny day, though thankfully there was no cliff in sight. There was no sign of Dad, either. Just Mom, running uphill along some street I'd never seen before, looking freaked-out and frantic. I barely caught a glimpse of palm trees in the background before the vision was gone.

"Hey," Cait blurted out. "I got one!"

"Me, too," I said, a little breathless as usual after a vision.

We both described what we'd seen, which turned out to be the exact same thing. "Palm trees?" Granny L said.

"Yeah," I said. "And come to think of it, I'm pretty sure Mom was wearing shorts. So, I guess it's probably not connected, since it's not shorts weather right now."

"Even if it were, where'd the palm trees come in?" Caitlyn wondered.

I shrugged. "Maybe we all go on vacation to Florida next summer. Whatever; it's not like we saw our father or anything."

Our grandmother looked troubled. "True," she said. "And it seems that touching your mother brought on a vision about her. But if you both saw the same thing, that means it's both good and bad, yes?"

"I guess," Caitlyn said, and I nodded.

Just then Granny L's cell phone buzzed. She checked it and sighed. "I have to go," she said, already starting to pack up the talismans. "I'll be in touch later."

Mom checked her watch. "Whoa, I need to leave too, or I'll be late for work. You two okay?"

We nodded, waiting until they'd both left. Then Cait turned and stared at me.

"What do you think this means?" she asked. "Do

you think that last vision is connected to the rest?"

Before I could respond, my phone burst into a snippet of a Sakiko Star song. It was Lavender calling.

"You'll never guess what Abby just found on eBay," she exclaimed. "It's a Sakiko heirloom!"

"Huh?" Okay, I'm probably Sakiko's number-one fan. But at the moment, I had other stuff on my mind. "Look Lav, can this wait? Because I'm kind of—"

"Seriously, check it out!" she babbled in my ear. "Just search on her name, and it's like the first thing that comes up, okay? Call me back when you find it."

She hung up. I was tempted to ignore her command, but I figured she'd keep bugging me until I looked. I didn't have the eBay app on my phone, so I stood up. "Where'd I leave my laptop?" I mumbled, heading into the living room.

Caitlyn followed me. "What are you doing?"

I told her what Lav had said. She rolled her eyes. "Sounds vitally important," she commented.

I rolled my eyes right back. "Don't try to be sarcastic, it doesn't work on you," I informed her.

My laptop was on the coffee table. I plopped onto the couch and opened it. Soon I was scrolling through a list of items for sale.

Caitlyn sat down next to me. "So what is it? One of Sakiko's teddy bears from that dumb video you're always making me watch?"

"No—I guess she's talking about this." I clicked on one of the items.

"A man's watch?" Cait sounded disinterested. "Weird."

"Yeah." I scanned the ad. "The seller claims she got it from her cousin. He's a photographer who found it in Sakiko's Dumpster."

"Why would Sakiko throw away a man's watch?"

I was still reading. "Wait, now I get it," I said. "It's not her watch—the seller pretty much admits that. It's something Sakiko's neighbor tossed in her Dumpster." When Cait stared at me blankly, I added, "You know—during their feud?" Still nothing. "Don't you ever pay attention to the news?"

"What news?"

"It's been going on for, like, months!" I exclaimed.

"Sakiko brought in a big Dumpster because she's having some work done on her house. Her weirdo neighbor keeps throwing his smelly garbage in there even though she told him to stop. I guess he even threw away his watch." I scanned the rest of the ad. "No, wait—not his watch. The seller thinks it probably belonged to his butler because it has the initials JTL on the back and the butler's name is Mr. Lincoln. She says here that it's a pretty fancy watch so she guesses Quentin Jeffers treats his staff well."

"Except when he's throwing away their stuff," Cait commented. Then she wrinkled her nose. "Quentin Jeffers—that's a funny name. Sounds kind of familiar for some reason, though . . ."

"They've probably mentioned it on the news," I said slowly. "Although I don't remember the Quentin part . . ." Suddenly I gasped. "Wait, that's it!"

My sister was staring at me now, her brown eyes wide. "Quentin Jeffers," she said. "QJ!"

"Yes!" I stared back at her, more than a few puzzle pieces suddenly clicking into place. Like those letters. And the inscription on the key chain. And

Sakiko Star's Dumpster full of blue feathers and sardine cans. And visions about shorts and palm trees and beaches . . .

Caitlyn grabbed my phone off the table where I'd dropped it. "We need to call Mom and Grandmother Lockwood," she said. "We might not have much time!"

13
CAITLYN

I FIDGETED IN my seat, peering out the plane window. There were only a few scattered clouds, making it easy to see the city of Los Angeles spread out below me, looking tiny and sort of unreal under the early morning sunshine.

In the seat next to me, Cassie let out a snorty little snore. I couldn't believe she'd slept through practically the whole flight.

"Wake up." I elbowed her. "We're getting ready to land."

She opened her eyes and yawned. "Huh?"

"I said, we're almost there." I shook my head. "I can't believe you can sleep at a time like this!"

"What can I say?" she joked drowsily. "Guess I'm just made for private air travel."

I glanced around the small plane. I had no idea how Grandmother Lockwood had managed to arrange this flight in less than a day, or how much it was costing her. What if this crazy theory that my sister and I had concocted yesterday turned out to be a big joke? Our grandmother would probably be furious.

"Do you think we're right about all this?" I asked Cassie quietly, shooting a look toward Mom and Grandmother Lockwood, who were seated across the way.

She sat up and stretched. "What else could it all mean?" she said. "Anyway, Mom and Granny L must believe it, since we're here."

She had a point. When our big brainstorm had hit us yesterday, we'd been afraid that the two of them wouldn't even listen to us. But not only had they listened, they'd been so sure that we were right that here we were—about to land in California after flying half the night!

"Anyway," Cassie said, sounding more awake with every passing moment, "we worked it all out, right? That watch didn't belong to Quentin Jeffers's butler—it belongs to our dad! JTL—John Thompson Lockwood."

"Yeah," I said, crossing my fingers and hoping she was right. "And if it ended up in Sakiko Star's Dumpster, it probably came from her neighbor—Quentin Jeffers."

"QJ," Cassie said with a nod. "Also known as the mysterious guy from the letters. He found out about the Sight and wanted Dad to come work for him . . ."

"And when he wouldn't, he kidnapped him." I shook my head. "I don't know, Cass. It still sounds a little crazy."

"Oh, it's totally wackadoodle," she said with a wave of her hand. "That doesn't mean it's not true, though. All the pieces fit."

"Right." I thought about that. "I guess it sort of

makes sense in a weird way. Sakiko's feud with her nutty neighbor . . ."

"The Dumpster diving paparazzi," Cassie continued. "Dad must have seen them out the window digging through Sakiko's garbage. And that gave him an idea about how to contact Mom."

I nodded. We'd worked all this out yesterday with Mom and Grandmother Lockwood. "The man in the suit from our visions must be Quentin's butler or something," I said. "Dad talked him into helping by planting the key chain and watch in Sakiko's Dumpster where someone would be sure to find them."

"There must have a been a note with the key chain," Cassie said. "Telling whoever found it to get it to Mom in San Antonio. Dad probably had no idea we'd moved to Aura."

"And that explains the words scratched on the back, too. It was Dad's way of telling Mom that he was still alive, and also where he was being held prisoner—in California. Heart you from UK to CA, right?" I glanced down at the landscape, which was coming closer into view as the plane circled downward. "I wonder why he didn't put a note with the watch, too."

"Maybe he did." Cassie shrugged. "It might have gotten lost, or drenched with sardine goo. Or maybe whoever found it ignored it and decided to sell the watch instead."

I figured she was probably right. She was probably also right about the reason the bad guys had tried to grab the key chain back. The butler had tossed some other trash into the Dumpster along with Dad's stuff to cover his tracks. Only that plan had backfired—Sakiko had noticed the smelly sardine cans, and the resulting feud had attracted public attention, which had tipped off Dad's captor.

Or something like that. We still weren't a hundred percent sure of all the details. But so far, everything matched up with our visions.

"What we saw in that first vision of Dad was probably him handing over the key chain to the butler," I mused.

Cassie leaned past me to peer out the window. "Right," she said. "And we also saw that guy with the ponytail digging through Sakiko's trash. He was probably the photographer who found the key chain. Or maybe the watch." She shot me a sidelong look. "And then you actually saw Sakiko herself in a vision. Jealous!"

I smiled. "I'm not jealous of your vision of the guy eating sardines," I joked. Then my smile faded. It really wasn't funny, now that I thought about it. If we were right, that old guy in the ratty robe had been holding our father prisoner for years—and might be getting ready to kill him right now!

A pang of fear shot through me. Maybe Cassie was thinking the same thing, or maybe it was that old twintuition kicking in again, but she caught my eye.

"We'll get there in time," she said, grabbing my hand and squeezing it. "Today is Sunday, right? And I'm pretty sure that's when my vision comes true— I saw a bunch of people coming out of a church, remember? So the earliest it could happen is today— and it's still really early."

I nodded, hoping she was right. That we would

arrive on time to stop what Cassie had seen yester-day. "I just hope my vision comes true," I said quietly. "The one of Grandmother Lockwood hugging Dad."

She squeezed my hand again. "It will."

I smiled at her. "Since when are you the optimis-tic twin?"

"I know, scary, right?"

AFTER WE LANDED, everything happened very fast. Mom tried to convince Cass and me to wait for them at the airport or the hotel they'd booked, but for once we didn't have to argue with her. That was because Grandmother Lockwood insisted on us coming along.

"We can't take any chances, Deidre," she said. "We may need the girls'—er—talents if things go wrong." She glanced around the airport suspiciously, but nobody was paying any attention to us.

"Fine." Mom didn't look happy, but she didn't argue either. "Then let's call the local precinct and find out where Sakiko Star lives."

"Not necessary, Mom," Cassie spoke up. She

pointed at a kiosk nearby. "Map of the stars. I'm sure it's on there."

She was right. Soon we were in a cab speeding into some hilly, super-ritzy part of LA near the ocean.

Cassie's eyes widened as we turned onto the block marked on the map. "That's it!" she squealed, bouncing up and down in her seat. "Sakiko Star's house—I'd recognize it anywhere!"

"That's right, missy." The cab driver glanced at us in the rearview mirror, managing to look both bored and amused at the same time. "You're a big fan, huh?"

"Thank you, sir." Grandmother Lockwood tossed a wad of cash over the seat. "That will be all."

We climbed out of the cab and it sped away. Grandmother Lockwood led the way to Quentin Jeffers's front door and rapped sharply on it.

"Here goes nothing," I whispered, reaching for Cassie's hand.

"Yeah," she murmured back.

For a second nothing happened. It was quiet, except for a lawn mower droning somewhere down the block. Not a sound came from inside except a muffled squawk.

"What was that?" Mom said. "Do you think it's John trying to call to us?"

"It didn't sound like a person," Cassie said. "More like a bird or maybe . . ."

She trailed off as the door finally swung open. I gasped at the familiar face in front of me—the butler! Even though I'd only seen him in visions, I would have known him anywhere. Well, except for . . .

"Whoa," Cassie said. "Check out that shiner!"

The butler had a black eye and a cut on his cheek that looked pretty fresh. His hair and clothes were much more disheveled than they'd ever looked in the visions.

"I'm Mrs. Verity Lockwood," our grandmother announced, drawing herself up to her full height. "I know my son John is here. Please take us to him at once."

The butler looked startled for a second. Then he sighed and shook his head. "So his crazy plan actually worked," he murmured. "Well, almost . . ."

"What are you talking about?" Mom demanded. "Where is he?"

The butler sighed again. "Sorry, but you're too late," he told us. "Mr. Jeffers knows everything. He just left to"—he gulped loudly—"er, to destroy the evidence."

14

CASSIE

"NO!" CAITLYN BLURTED out, her face going pale.

Mom and Granny L both started talking, arguing with the butler. But I was running through my vision in my head.

"Quiet," I blurted out. I guessed Mom and Granny L were startled enough to obey. They both stared at me as I took a step toward the butler. "Is there a church near here?" I asked. "White, modern-looking, but with a cross on top and a big, round stained-glass window?"

The butler stared at me. "Why do you ask, miss?"

"Because that's where this crazy Quentin guy is taking our dad," I told him.

"Cass . . . ," Caitlyn murmured.

But I'd had enough of secrets. I glared at the butler. "Look, my dad has been a prisoner here for years, right?" I said. "So you must know he can see the future sometimes. Well, so can we." I gestured to my sister and myself. "And that's why we need you to tell us how to get to that church!"

The butler gulped, but he didn't look all that surprised, which meant I was probably right—he knew about the Sight. "I'm sorry, miss. I already told you—you're too late. Besides, if I told you . . ." His fingers crept to the cut on his cheek.

Mom stepped forward. "Enough," she snapped. "If you know where this church is, you'd better tell us or I'll arrest you for aiding and abetting a criminal."

The butler didn't look particularly scared by her threat. I guessed it was because he was way more scared of crazy Quentin than anything else. Had he whacked him with that cane I'd seen in my vision?

Quentin was bad news—that much was obvious by now. "Please," I added.

"Yes—please tell us." Caitlyn's voice quivered. "He's our dad, and we haven't seen him since we were babies."

"Oh, dear." The butler looked torn. Finally he nodded, seeming to reach a decision. "All right, then," he said. "You need to head up the street that way, and then . . ."

We all listened carefully to the directions. It sounded as if the church—and the cliff—were at least a mile away. I just hoped we had time to get there before my vision came true.

I guessed Granny L had the same worry. She'd stayed surprisingly quiet through all this, but now she spun on her heel. "Let's go," she said in her bossy British voice. "We don't have much time."

We all took off up the street at a run. "Did he say the turn was three blocks or four past the purple house?" Caitlyn panted as she ran beside me.

"Four, I think." I glanced over my shoulder. "I wish he'd come with us."

"We're lucky he told us anything at all," Mom

said breathlessly. "As it is, he stands to lose his job when Mr. Jeffers finds out."

"Or maybe his life," I added. "I mean, you have to be a total psycho to keep someone prisoner all these years, right?"

Nobody had a response to that. The street was getting steeper, and I spotted several gulls wheeling overhead nearby. Just like in my vision . . .

"I think it's that way," I gasped out when we reached an intersection. I pointed in the direction of the gulls—up a stone-paved trail leading into a little park-like area.

"What?" Mom skidded to a stop. "But the butler said to follow this street all the way to the shore."

"Maybe he's thinking of how he'd get there by driving," Cait suggested. "Besides, we're not actually going to that church, remember? So Cassie's way could be a shortcut to the actual spot we want."

Mom looked dubious. Granny L didn't say anything—she was leaning over, hands on her knees and panting. She was actually pretty fit for an old lady, but I wasn't sure she'd be able to keep up much longer.

"I have an idea," I said. "Cait and I will go this way, and you two go that way. We should meet up in the right spot eventually."

"Good. Come on!" My sister took off without waiting for them to answer. I sprinted after her.

I could hear Mom calling after us, sounding anxious. But we didn't slow down, and she didn't follow, so I guess she was down with the plan.

Cait and I didn't talk as we ran this time. The trail led up a steep hill, and then ended, but I could see the crest of the hill just ahead over the grass. Right before we reached the crest, church bells started to ring somewhere off to the left.

"Hurry!" I blurted out, putting on a last burst of speed.

At the top of the hill, we stopped short. A few yards ahead the ground suddenly dropped away, and the Pacific Ocean lay before us, glittering under the morning sun. Caitlyn let out a gasp, but it wasn't because she was admiring the view.

"There!" she cried.

I looked to the right, where she was pointing. It was our father! He was older than in that wedding photo, of course, but I would have recognized him anywhere. He was standing with his back to the edge of the cliff, hands up in front of him and eyes wide.

I also recognized the person standing there leaning on a cane and pointing a gun at our dad. Quentin Jeffers—the sardine-eating old man from my vision.

"Stop!" I yelled.

Quentin whirled around, looking startled. "Hey!" he said. "Who are you?"

Dad blinked at us. Then his jaw dropped. "Cassie—Caitlyn?" he called. "Is it—am I seeing things? Is it really you?"

That stopped me short for a second. He hadn't seen us since we were little more than babies. Not in person, anyway.

He half smiled, seeming to guess what I was thinking. "I've seen photos of you two online," he said. "Quentin sometimes lets me . . ." His voice trailed off, and his eyes bounced back to the guy with the gun.

Oh, yeah, right. The guy with the gun. This was

no time for trading stories.

Caitlyn took a cautious step forward. "Mr. Jeffers?" she said in her best talking-to-adults voice. "Please—please don't do this."

"Girls, stay back," our father called. "I don't want you involved in this."

"We're already involved." I shot a look around, wishing that Mom and Granny L would show up soon. What was taking them so long? "Why are you doing this, anyway?"

Quentin frowned. "None of your business," he snapped. Then he waved the gun around. "But if you must know, it's because your father has become more of a liability to me than an asset." He glared at Dad. "If only he'd cooperated instead of concocting his silly escape plan, none of this would have had to happen."

"Well, it wouldn't have happened if you hadn't kidnapped him, either," Caitlyn exclaimed.

"Girls, please!" Dad sounded frantic now. "Back off. You don't know what he's capable of."

Quentin smirked. "That's right, girls," he said.

"Listen to your daddy, okay? Once he's out of the way, maybe the three of us can go back to my house and have a little chat."

"No!" Dad cried. "Girls, run! You can't let him—"

"Shut up." Quentin cocked the gun.

I froze. I'd heard that sound plenty of times—Mom had taught Caitlyn and me to shoot a couple of years ago, and still took us to the range to practice now and then. Not to mention all the action shows and movies I'd seen over the years.

But this was different. Scarier. *Way* scarier.

"Stop, please!" I cried. "What if Cait and I promise to go back with you? Will you let him go?"

"No!" Dad cried again. "Don't do it!"

Quentin chuckled. "Don't worry, John," he told Dad. "There's nothing your daughters can say to make it worth leaving you alive. It's time for you to die—just like the rest of the world thought you did a decade ago."

He lifted the gun, sighting down it—right at Dad! My heart pounded. We had to do something! But what? How could we get through to Quentin?

He had all the power over us, and we had none over him. Unless . . .

Suddenly a detail from my vision popped into my head—along with something Cait had described from one of hers. And then an idea started to form. Would it work? There was only one way to find out.

"Stop!" I shouted again. "Seriously, dude. Because we're holding your beloved pet parrot hostage. And we'll feed it to Sakiko Star's dog if you hurt our dad!"

15
CAITLYN

AT FIRST I thought Cassie had gone crazy-loco, babbling about parrots and dogs. But Quentin Jeffers blanched and lowered his gun slightly.

"You're lying," he snapped, leaning hard on his cane. "You don't really have Bluebeard."

But I could hear the worry in his voice. I guessed Cass could, too, because she actually smiled.

"It's true, dude. Our mother has him back at your house. Now let him go, or the birdie gets it." She drew one finger across her throat to illustrate.

Suddenly I caught on. That squawk we'd heard from inside Quentin's house—it had to be the parrot I'd seen in my visions! And Cassie had seen the butler sweeping up blue feathers in one of her visions. The parrot must belong to Quentin!

"Don't hurt Bluebeard." The old man sounded frantic now. "He's innocent!"

"So's our dad." Cassie's voice was steely. "Let him go, and we'll give Bluebeard back."

Quentin frowned, his eyes shooting from us to Dad and back again. "Fine," he snapped. "But first I want to see that he's safe." He waved the gun toward Dad. "We'll all go together."

It was a tense walk back to Quentin's house. At least most of it was downhill. Quentin insisted that Dad walk right ahead of him, and that Cassie and I stay on the other side of the street "so you can't try anything funny," he'd explained with a suspicious glare.

"What does he think we're going to do?" Cassie whispered as we trudged along, doing our best to stay exactly opposite the two men.

"I don't know," I replied quietly. "I just wish Mom was here."

Cassie glanced over at the two men again. Then she stuck her hand in the pocket of her shorts. "Let me know if Quentin looks over here," she hissed.

"What are you doing?" I shot the old man a nervous look. If he thought we were trying anything funny . . .

"Texting Mom," Cass whispered so quietly I wasn't sure I'd heard her right.

Texting her without looking at her phone, or even taking it out of her pocket? I was a little dubious. But if anyone could do that, it was my sister, the texting fool.

I didn't worry about it for long, anyway. Because we were already almost back to Quentin's house. He could move pretty fast, even with that cane.

"Stay back, girls," our father called as we started across the street.

"No, come along, girls," Quentin said. "You have to tell your mother to release Bluebeard, and then we'll talk about what happens next." He stepped

closer to Dad, pointing the gun at his head. "Inside—
ladies first."

Cassie and I traded a nervous look. You didn't
have to have a cop for a mother to know that it's
never a good idea to go into a homicidal stranger's
house. But what choice did we have?

We pushed open the big front door and stepped
into the spacious marble-floored foyer. Quentin followed, poking Dad along at the muzzle of the gun.

"Sir!" The butler hurried in from another room
with a large blue parrot perched on his shoulder.

Quentin gasped. "Bluebeard!" he cried. "You're
safe!" Then he turned and glared at us, realization
dawning on his pinched face. He lifted his cane and
pointed it at us like a huge, accusing finger. "You
kids lied to me. That means the deal's off!"

"No!" I blurted out. I spun to face the butler, who
looked confused. "Help us—please! He's crazy!"

The butler didn't meet my eye. "Here you go, sir,"
he said softly, stroking the parrot and then passing
it over to Quentin. "Bluebeard was eagerly awaiting
your return."

Quentin settled the large bird on his narrow shoulder. "There, there, my love," he murmured, letting his cane fall against his side so he could reach up and scratch Bluebeard on the chest. "Everything's going to be all right now."

"Easy for him to say," Cassie muttered. Then she cleared her throat. "So why'd you do it, Quen—er, Mr. Jeffers?" she asked. "What made you decide to kidnap our dad, anyway?"

The old man glanced at her, looking amused. "Nice try, young lady," he said. "This isn't *Scooby-Doo*. You meddling kids aren't going to get me talking so you can concoct some crazy escape plan. This is real life."

His words hit me hard, because he was right. This *was* real life. And that was our real father standing there in front of us for the first time in more than ten years. Was this really how our reunion with him was going to end?

"Please," I blurted out. "Can't we just hug him?"

"What?" Quentin turned and stared at me.

"Our dad." I swallowed hard, feeling tears stinging my eyes. "We haven't seen him practically our whole lives, and if you're going to—you know . . ." I waved a hand at the gun. "I mean, can't we just have one hug first?"

I expected him to say no—maybe let out an evil laugh like the villain in a movie. But he actually looked touched.

"Oh—well," he mumbled. "Now, if you're talking about absent fathers, I suppose I know what that's like, so . . ." He cleared his throat. "All right, one hug each. That's it." He waved the gun. "And don't try anything funny, or your father won't be the only one who gets it!"

He stepped back out of the way. For a second, Dad just stood there gazing at us. Then, suddenly, we were all in motion.

I felt Cassie's elbow connect with my rib cage, and I'm pretty sure I poked Dad in the ear with my thumb. But nobody minded as we tangled ourselves up in a big, crazy family hug.

"Oh, girls!" Dad's voice sounded choked up and hoarse. "I hoped I'd see you again one day, but I was starting to think . . ."

"We thought you were dead," Cassie mumbled.

"All this time, we thought you were dead!"

I didn't say anything. I couldn't. It was way too overwhelming. Instead, I just hugged my father as tightly as I could, wishing I never had to let go . . .

But Quentin only gave us a few seconds. "All right, that's enough," he said. "One hug—that was the deal. Now back off."

"No!" Cassie moaned.

"Please!" I cried.

But Dad gently disentangled us. "It's okay, girls." His voice was steady now as he backed up a few steps. He glanced toward the front door. "They can go now, right, Quentin?"

Quentin frowned. "No," he said. "They stay." He smirked. "I'm sure they'd love to hear their daddy's voice for a few more seconds, even if it's just you crying and begging for your life."

Dad shrugged. "I have nothing more to say to you, Quentin."

Quentin looked surprised. But then he shrugged, too. "Fine. Then prepare to die."

"I'm ready." Dad straightened to his full height.

"Even death has to be better than spending another second trapped here in this nightmare of a mansion, dealing with your crazy whims and experiments."

I tensed up and turned my face away, expecting to hear the gun go off. Instead, I heard Quentin let out a loud sniff. "What are you talking about?" he said, sounding insulted. "Of all the ungrateful . . . I've done everything I could to make you comfortable here. You had only the best of everything money could buy—food, clothing, this beautiful place to live . . ."

As he turned slightly, waving his gun toward the fancy chandelier or whatever, I saw my chance. The parrot wobbled slightly on the old man's shoulder, fighting to stay balanced.

I darted forward and grabbed the bird's long blue tail feathers, giving them a good yank. Bluebeard let out a deafening squawk, scrabbling to regain his balance on his bony perch but quickly giving up and flying off in a rush of wings.

"Bluebeard!" Quentin cried, lunging after the bird.

I grabbed Cassie by the hand. "Dad, run!" I shouted.

We raced for the door—and almost collided with Mom as she ran in, service revolver in hand! Grandmother Lockwood was a few steps behind her.

"Freeze!" Mom shouted in her best cop voice. "Hands where I can see them!"

Quentin, Dad, and the butler all stopped short, sticking their hands in the air. Mom bustled over and plucked the gun out of Quentin's hand.

Meanwhile Dad's eyes went wide. "D-Deidre?" he stammered, lowering his hands.

"Hello, John." Mom's eyes went soft for a second. But then Quentin started to lower his hands, too, and she spun to face him, instantly back in police mode. "Quentin Jeffers, you're under arrest," she barked out. "You have the right to remain silent . . ."

As she recited the Miranda rights, I heard a commotion from the doorway. "What's going on over here?" a female voice demanded.

Cassie turned and her jaw dropped. "Sakiko?" she squealed. "Oh my gosh, I'm your number-one fan!"

Okay, that was yet another face from a vision I was seeing in real life. Sakiko Star was staring in at us, looking annoyed and confused at the same time. Everyone started talking at once, and out of nowhere about a zillion paparazzi appeared and started snapping photos of us, Sakiko, Dad, Quentin, and even Bluebeard, who was perched on the chandelier as if it was the world's biggest, fanciest, craziest, most expensive bird swing.

Which was probably the least weird thing that had happened all day.

16

CASSIE

A COUPLE OF hours later, the whole family finally got a chance to relax and talk in the swanky hotel suite Granny L had rented.

That's right. The whole family. Me, my sister, our mom. The grandmother we hadn't even known about until a few weeks ago.

And our dad.

"This is amazing," Caitlyn burbled for the millionth time. "I can't believe we're all here together!"

Mom shook her head. "It really is hard to believe."

She was sitting on the sofa with Dad. The two of them had barely stopped holding hands since we'd walked out of the LA police station a little while earlier. Cute, right? A little weird, too. I wasn't used to seeing Mom looking so happy—almost giddy. Which was so not a word I would normally use to describe her.

But whatever. This was definitely an unusual occasion.

"So I still don't get it," I said. "How'd that scrawny old guy manage to take you prisoner in the first place? Hired ninjas or something?"

Dad chuckled. "Not exactly." Then his expression went serious again. "It all started with a vision."

"Ugh." I rolled my eyes. "I should have known! That's how all our troubles start lately."

Caitlyn laughed. "Not necessarily," she told me. "Some of our visions have led to good stuff. Like this." She beamed at Dad.

"Your visions, maybe," I reminded her, my hand straying up to touch the talisman around my neck. "Mine only show the bad stuff, remember?"

"What?" Dad leaned forward. "What do you mean?"

We'd filled him in on a few things over the past couple of hours, including the fact that both Caitlyn and I had inherited the Sight. But we hadn't had time to cover all the details yet.

"Yeah, that's how it seems to break down between us." I gestured at Cait. "She sees good stuff happening, I see bad stuff."

"Really? Wow." Dad stroked his chin with the hand that wasn't clutched in Mom's. "Bummer for you, Cassie."

"Tell me about it."

"Only it's not that simple," Caitlyn protested. "Sometimes it gets all mixed up—like in those visions we had when Lavender got kidnapped. That was all bad, really, but I saw some of it, too."

"Only the parts Lav thought were good, like when she thought she was going to a sample sale," I said. Then I blinked at Dad, who looked confused. "But never mind that. You were going to tell us how you ended up that nut's prisoner."

"Right." He nodded. "I had a vision about you girls, back when you were just toddlers."

"You did?" Mom said. "You never told me that."

Dad bit his lip. "That's because of what I saw. It was the girls crying and screaming as someone dragged them into a car. I was afraid it might be Quentin."

"What?" I leaned forward in my chair. "Quentin? Why?"

"He'd contacted me just before that," Dad explained. "Somehow he'd figured out the Lock-wood legacy—I still don't know how."

"We do," Caitlyn said with a gasp.

"We do?" I stared at her. "Want to fill us in?"

"It was the diary!" Caitlyn sounded excited. She glanced at Granny L, who was wandering around the room, occasionally stopping to touch Dad on the shoulder. "Right? You said it was out of the family's possession for a while, and I saw that post about it on the Internet . . ."

Then I remembered. Caitlyn had done some online research and found a message board where someone mentioned the Lockwoods. The poster claimed to have found a diary in some junk shop somewhere—one that had belonged to Dad and other Lockwoods before him. We'd already figured out that it was the same one Granny L had been using as a talisman.

Granny L nodded thoughtfully. "That makes sense," she agreed. "Although we still don't know how the diary ended up out in the world."

Dad looked startled. "Wait—are you talking about my diary? The little leather one I used to carry around?" He gulped. "Oh, man . . ."

"What?" Mom squeezed his hand. "What's wrong, John?"

"This is all my fault!" He passed a hand over his face. "I lost that diary on a train once—someone must have found it, and somehow it ended up with Quentin."

"So that's how he found out about the Sight?" I said.

"I suppose so." Dad sighed, leaning back on the sofa. "And once he did, he was determined to use my power to rule the world, or live forever, or make money—actually I'm not really sure what he thought he could do with it. But if there's power to be had, some people will do anything to grab it."

"So wait," I said. "What did your vision have to do with all that? The one about us."

"It happened a couple of months after Quentin first contacted me," Dad explained. "He was trying to convince me to work with him to figure out how the Sight works—he was sure he could expand my powers, maybe figure out how to re-create them . . ." He shook his head. "Naturally, I said thanks but no thanks. So then he started making threats."

Mom looked grim. "The girls?"

"Yes. And you. He seemed so desperate—I wasn't sure what he'd do," Dad said. "Then I had that vision while I was kissing you girls good night, and, well . . ."

"You wanted to protect your daughters," Granny L finished for him, sounding angry and proud all at once. "Oh, John!"

"What else could I do?" Dad shrugged. "I struck a

deal with Quentin. At least I thought we had a deal."

"What do you mean?" Caitlyn asked. "What kind of deal?"

"Quentin probably double-crossed Dad somehow," I told her. "Right?"

Dad smiled ruefully. "Right." He turned to Mom. "Remember the fishing trip I took to Canada with my mates from school? And the business trip to Seattle a few months after that?"

"Let me guess," Mom said. "Those were actually trips here to see Quentin."

He nodded. "We'd agreed that I would come over to LA for a week or so at a time as often as possible— minimum four times per year." He grimaced. "But after the second trip, he saw some random comment online and got paranoid, thinking I was spilling all his secrets or something."

"And then you left again, supposedly to take the flying lessons you'd always talked about," Mom said softly. "Only that time, you never came back."

There was a moment of silence. All those years lost. Stolen by a paranoid old man.

"Anyway," Dad said at last. "Quentin has plenty of resources, so it was easy for him to fake that small plane crash. Apparently, nobody was actually hurt—well, except for the plane, of course. But everyone thought . . ."

He didn't finish. He didn't have to. We all knew the rest. Quentin had decided to make sure Dad would never spill his secrets—or leave—again.

"Too bad Quentin didn't realize that the Sight doesn't answer to anyone, no matter how much money they have," I said. "I mean, it's not like Cait and I have any idea how to control it."

"We're getting better, though. At least a little." She smiled at our grandmother. "Grandmother Lockwood has been helping us."

"Is that right, Mother?" Dad smiled at Granny L. "I'm glad you found the girls in time. That's why I came up with my escape plan now, after all these years. I hadn't tried before then because I was afraid of what Quentin might do to my family even if I did manage to get away. But once I realized that the girls would be coming into their powers . . ." He glanced at us. "Although I assumed it would only be one of them."

"Surprise!" I said, which made everyone laugh, even Granny L—a little.

"It took a while to convince Nicholas—he's the butler—to help me," Dad continued. "He was always very kind, but he was also afraid to cross Quentin. Everyone who works for him is." He shuddered. "But finally we hit on our plan. I was afraid it might not work . . ."

"It probably wouldn't have if not for the girls' visions," Mom spoke up. "They're the ones who figured out where to look for you."

"Really?" Dad smiled at Cait and me. "That's my girls."

For some reason, out of everything that had happened that day, that was what did me in. That one little stupid phrase: *That's my girls.* Still, tears came to my eyes as I finally realized what was happening here. I had my father back!

"Scoot over, Mom," I said, hopping up and hurrying over to the sofa. "You've been hogging Dad this whole time. Give someone else a turn, okay?"

Mom laughed and moved aside. "Hey, me too!" Caitlyn exclaimed, racing over and flinging herself onto the sofa on Dad's other side. "Daddy sandwich!" she exclaimed, hugging him.

"In case you haven't noticed, Dad, I'm the cool one and she's the dork," I informed him. Then I hugged him, too.

And that's when the vision came. Buzzing filled my head, and my real father—my real, live, long-lost-but-now-returned father—faded away, replaced by a vivid version of him standing in a fancy room.

As in, a *really* fancy room. It was the size of the Aura Middle School auditorium, pretty much, with lots of gorgeous furniture and a huge Persian rug covering part of the marble floor. What looked like real oil paintings of old-fashioned people lined the walls, and there was also a British flag hanging by the window. And did I mention the enormous Christmas tree over by the fireplace?

Oh, and Caitlyn was there, too, along with Mom and Granny L and a bunch of other people I didn't recognize but was pretty sure I might be related to, all looking as happy as could be . . .

"Whoa!" Cait exclaimed, breaking the spell.

I blinked, the vision gone as fast as it had come. "Did you see it, too?" I asked.

"Yeah." She looked worried for a second. "Wait— if we both saw it, that means it's going to be both good and bad, right?"

Dad and the others looked confused. "What's going on?" Mom asked. "What did you see?"

I ignored her question, at least for the moment, turning over Caitlyn's comment in my head. Nothing about what I'd just seen had seemed bad at all. Then again, when it came to the Sight, it could be hard to tell . . .

"I know," I said, reaching past Dad to squeeze my sister's hand. "It's probably one of those moments when everything is so great that you never want it to end, so knowing it will end is the bad part."

She smiled and squeezed back. "Yeah. Kind of like right now."